WOOING THE WIDOWER COPY

ELLE E. KAY

FAITH WRITES PUBLISHING

Wooing the Widower

CHRISTMAS IN REDEMPTION RIDGE

Copyright © 2023 Elle E. Kay

All rights reserved.

Faith Writes Publishing

PO BOX 494

BENTON PA 17814-0494

Ebook ISBN: 978-1-950240-35-7

Paperback ISBN: 978-1-950240-39-5

CHAPTER 1

MARGIE WAS READY FOR adventure. She made the turn at the sign for Redemption Ranch and followed the long drive. She passed pastures filled with horses then a riding ring where a young man led around a horse with a boy on its back. The massive stone front of the lodge was reflected in the lake, giving it an ethereal feel. Smaller adobe buildings and stables could be seen beyond the main lodge. And the rugged mountains stood sentry over it all.

Her son-in-law had suggested the place. She'd initially booked a month at a dude ranch thinking the immersive experience would be beneficial, but Gage convinced her not to go through with it. This place was supposed to have it all. Both the rustic outdoor experience and all the little luxuries she appreciated. She smiled as she pulled her Mazda SUV into a parking spot. This was going to be a blast.

She drew in a breath of crisp air mixed with the scent of hay and horses, smells she recognized but had rarely been exposed to. She'd always wanted to learn how to ride horses, and if all went according to plan, she'd be old hat at it before she headed back home come the end of the month.

A man with salt-and-pepper hair stepped out into the

bright sunshine, and she grinned. Her daughter's father-in-law. Martin Charles Buchanan. His friends called him Chaz, but she'd never been counted among the honored few.

"Welcome." He joined her at her vehicle, and his hazel eyes met hers. He was quite the looker. She never did understand why he hadn't remarried after his wife died. The man was a catch. "Gage said you'd be checking in today."

She pressed the button on her key fob, and her hatch popped open. When she reached in to grab the handle of her suitcase, Chaz did the same, and their hands brushed. Smiling, she stepped back. Since she'd been living alone for so long, she was used to doing everything herself, but saw no reason to reject help when offered.

He hauled it from her trunk and grabbed the other two pieces of luggage she'd brought. "I'll take these to your room."

"Thank you." She followed as he led the way through the lodge. Earthy shades of terracotta and turquoise echoed the beauty of the surrounding landscape. "It's great to see you again. How do you like ranch life?"

"It's okay."

"Ever miss the boardroom?"

"Sometimes."

"How are Carly and Thomas? I haven't seen them in ages."

"Good." He gestured for her to enter her room.

Stepping inside, she surveyed the space, taking in the cozy blend of southwest charm and modern comforts. A decorative clay pot rested on the dresser, and an Aztec-patterned blanket lay across the bottom of the bed. By the window sat a rocking chair. Another seating area surrounded a television. Through the bathroom door, she noticed a luxurious jacuzzi bathtub. Yes. This place would be a dream. "It's gorgeous."

"My half-brother Barry and his wife Connie put a lot of blood and sweat into this place. It's one of a kind."

"I appreciate you carrying my things in for me, Mr. Buchanan."

"We don't stand on formalities at the ranch, Margie. Call me Chaz."

She couldn't hold back her grin. All the years of working with him on real estate deals for his business, and he'd never suggested first names. But they were family now. Sort of. "I'll do that, Chaz. Will I see you later?"

He nodded and tipped his hat then headed down the hall.

～

ON MONDAY MORNING, CHAZ closed the door to the tack room and inhaled deeply. Leather and hay. Better than the manure the young ranch hands had shoveled out of the stalls earlier. After a quick inventory, he was satisfied they had enough gear for the overnight camping trip scheduled for Friday and Saturday. According to Barry, it was a popular event. A chance for guests to experience a brief, but authentic taste of ranch life. He was tagging along as their campfire cook since the guy who usually handled the meals was in the hospital following a bad fall.

Barry walked in with his ever-present clipboard. "Hey." He grinned. "We've got a full roster for Friday's trip."

Chaz grunted and refolded a saddle blanket.

"Margie signed up." Barry chuckled.

"Yeah? So?" Chaz frowned and threw a look over his shoulder at the ginger-haired woman brushing down one of the horses. "Leona is, too. Doesn't mean a thing."

"Of course, it does. Leona's been around livestock her whole life. Margie doesn't even know how to ride a horse. You could offer her some private lessons."

"Why would I do that? You have plenty of people on staff for that."

"She's a beautiful woman. Single, too."

"And my son's mother-in-law. Don't get any crazy ideas of fixing us up. It'd just be weird."

"The woman came here looking for adventure. Who better to show her adventure than the former CEO of Freedom Mountaineering? Is there anything you don't know about Colorado's great outdoors?"

He made a noncommittal sound and stalked back into the barn. Horses were far less talkative than his brother. It was bad enough he'd tricked him into relocating to Redemption Ranch claiming he needed help, but now he was going to try to set him up with the most unsuitable woman in the world. A woman who loved to hear herself talk. Casey's mother. No. Not a chance. Never in a million years could he ever see himself with Margie Crawford.

MARGIE LOOKED AT THE enormous beast and swallowed hard. Maybe riding a horse wasn't such a good idea after all. She reached out a hand and gave the horse a pat on the neck.

"Daisy here is a gentle giant. Don't let her size scare you, she's perfect for beginners," Paul said. He was the ranch's head wrangler but had volunteered to give her lessons when she'd run into him the night before. She suspected his willingness to help her might have something to do with her age and gender. There probably weren't too many women over fifty hanging around the ranch. She wasn't necessarily opposed to the idea of kindling a new romance, but her primary purpose in booking this trip was to learn how to ride horses. Anything more was a bonus, but she was going back to Freedom in a month, so unless a man was willing to relocate, it would never work.

Drawing in a deep breath, she climbed up onto the step and then set her foot in the stirrup and swung herself onto the animal.

"Okay, now grab the reins, but hold them loosely." He handed her the reins and kept his eyes locked on hers longer than necessary.

"Like this?"

"That's right." He smiled. "You're doing great. Now sit there a moment, talk to her, and get to know each other. It's important to bond with your horse."

After a few minutes, he went back into instruction mode and showed her how to use her feet to exert gentle pressure to show the horse where she wanted to go.

When the lesson concluded, she climbed down from the horse, and thanked Paul.

"You're a natural, Margie. Would you care to schedule another lesson?"

She glanced toward the barn and noticed a cowboy in a straw hat, chewing a piece of hay. It only took a moment for her to recognize Chaz. She smiled. He'd traded in business suits for jeans and a cowboy hat, and the new look fit him perfectly. Like he was born to it. Maybe he was, he did say Barry was his brother. She'd have to ask him about his background.

"Margie?"

Turning back to Paul, she felt her face warm. She'd been caught staring at Chaz. "Sorry. Distracted."

He chuckled. "I can see that. The new guy is going to give me a run for my money."

"I'd love another lesson."

"That's more like it." He grinned. "Tomorrow morning. Nine o'clock?"

"Perfect."

∽

CHAZ' GUT CLENCHED AS he watched Margie dismount Daisy, the Belgian Draft horse Paul had chosen for her riding lesson. Maverick and Gideon usually handled riding lessons and pony patrol. There was only one reason he would've chosen to teach her himself. The annoying gnawing sensation in his stomach made no sense. Chaz wasn't jealous. No way. It was good that the head wrangler took the time to make Margie feel welcome. And if more came from their interactions, then he would applaud whatever developed.

Margie pushed her chin-length blonde hair out of her face, and her gaze settled on him. He turned away, breaking eye contact. When he looked again, she was shaking hands with her instructor. A moment later, she strolled over to him. "Been standing here long?"

"Long enough to see you getting comfortable with your horse."

"Missed you at supper last night," she said.

"Ate in town."

"Oh. I thought you'd be around."

"Went to Charlie's Hardware, so I grabbed a bite at Flapjacks."

"Flapjacks? Sounds like a breakfast place."

"Ummhmm."

"Maybe you could show me around town sometime."

"Yeah, maybe." He adjusted his hat.

"Want to take a walk? I saw something in the brochure about the Triple R Chapel. I was hoping to see it."

"I guess I can show you. It's not far."

As they walked, Margie filled the silence. "Seems like Casey and Gage are making a real difference in Bangladesh. Don't you think so?"

"Ummhmm."

"How is it going with Carly running Freedom Mountaineering? Are the expansion plans continuing?"

"Yeah. She's got it under control." His girl had stepped up to the plate. There was a time when she'd wanted nothing to do with his company and had resented him trying to convince her to get involved in running it, but after being diagnosed with Postural Orthostatic Tachycardia Syndrome, she'd settled into her new role as CEO, which required her to be on her feet far less than her working as a sous chef. She still enjoyed cooking, but didn't seem to miss Liberty Grille's busy kitchen.

"How about you? Are you happy with your move to Redemption Ranch?"

Was he? Nobody had asked him that before. "I guess. The ranch I grew up on wasn't far from here. A few years after my dad died, my mother remarried Barry's father. So, my last year of high school was spent here."

"Did you play sports in high school?"

"Rodeo. I rode bulls." He nodded at Leona as she passed them on horseback. They'd dated back in school. That was a long time ago. He'd been surprised to see her at Redemption Ranch when she'd grown up on a ranch herself. He figured it was nostalgia for the glory days. Growing older made him think back to his youth a lot. Sometimes he wondered if he would do things differently if given another chance.

"Goodness. You are a reckless one, aren't you? Now I know where Gage gets his wild side."

"Wild? Gage?" He'd never thought of his son that way.

"I've heard some of his Army stories. The boy was no slacker."

"No." He chuckled. "He held his own."

8

They reached the chapel, and she looked at the steepled roof. "It's beautiful." Once inside, she turned in a slow circle and admired the glass structure. Sunshine streamed in the floor-to-ceiling glass windows. "Wow. The light in here is amazing."

His gaze locked on the large wooden cross in the front of the space. "Yes. It's like heaven came down and filled the space."

"That may be the longest sentence I've heard you mutter since I arrived."

"I talk."

"Sure, you do." She chuckled.

"Barry said you were joining the camping trip."

"I am. I cannot wait. It sounds like so much fun."

"It's quite a bit of riding for a novice. Are you sure you're up for it? You may get sore."

"Paul said I could use Daisy. He's going to give me lessons a couple more times before Friday so that I'll be ready."

His gut churned again, informing him that no matter what he told himself, it did bother him that Margie would be spending so much time with Paul. He could offer to give her lessons himself, but doing so to keep her from spending time with the head ranch hand would be childish. Besides, he wasn't looking for a relationship. Especially not with his son's mother-in-law.

CHAPTER 2

LAVENDER AND EUCALYPTUS GREETED Margie as she pushed open the door to Redemption Spa. The spa's decor mirrored the adobe-style charm of the ranch, but it took luxury to a whole new level.

A receptionist looked up at her. "Good morning, do you have an appointment?"

"Yes. Margie Crawford. I'm booked for the full experience."

The girl had a twinkle in her eye. "You're in for a treat. We'll start you off with your massage." The girl came out from behind the counter and beckoned her to follow. "Just through here."

After a massage and a facial, she was brought into another room and a manicurist placed her right hand in warm water. "Are you enjoying your time at Redemption Ranch, Ms. Crawford?".

"Call me Margie." She beamed. "I love it here. The horses, especially. I always wanted to learn how to ride."

"And have you taken lessons?"

"Yes. I had my second lesson this morning. I'll be going on the camping trip Friday, so I'm hoping to learn all the basics beforehand."

"That trip is fun. I went on it with my siblings a couple of years ago."

Margie was looking forward to it. And it might be the perfect opportunity to get Chaz to open up. He'd always been such a closed book, but maybe the forced proximity would encourage him to share. It was probably wishful thinking, but she'd give it her best effort.

Following a beautiful French manicure, she was sure to ruin within hours of leaving the spa, she had her hair washed, and then took the seat the stylist gestured her toward. "What did you have in mind?" The younger woman grinned. "I heard you were feeling adventurous."

"Not that adventurous. Let's not do anything too drastic."

"How about we cut in some additional layers to give your hair a little more movement and bring out that natural wave of yours? And lowlights might be nice, too."

She nodded. "Sounds good."

CHAZ STRODE DOWN THE gravel drive toward the ranch office. There were some last-minute details he needed to go over with his niece, Cassie, before the camping trip. She kept the place running smoothly with her attention to detail, but he'd noticed a few irregularities in the inventory, and wanted to give her a heads up. He could pick up the items they were missing, but if employees were failing to sign out items, or worse, if someone was stealing from them, she needed to know.

The door to the lodge opened, and he spotted Margie stepping out. He walked to where she stood shielding her eyes from the brilliant sunshine. Her cropped hair looked different; it framed her face in a flattering way and had a bounce to it he hadn't noticed before. And those eyes. They were so blue.

"Hi, Chaz." She smiled.

"Hey. You look ... I don't know. Different."

"Is that good or bad?"

"Good. I mean, not that you normally look bad." He couldn't stop his own stammering. His foot was firmly in his mouth, and he couldn't seem to remove it.

She laughed. A clear bright sound that made him want to make her repeat it.

"You look beautiful."

"Thank you. I guess they know what they're doing at the spa."

"What are you up to now?"

"Just thought I'd go for a walk. Care to join?"

"I'm afraid I'm working, but maybe another time."

She headed away from the lodge, and he smiled to himself. When he entered the office, he was whistling a tune, and Cassie gave him a curious look.

"Don't even start on me."

"Wouldn't dream of it." She folded her hands on the desk. "What's up?"

~

ON WEDNESDAY NIGHT, MARGIE pushed open the heavy wooden doors of Redemption Bible Church. Most of the seats were taken, but she tucked herself into a half-empty pew near the back of the church. As the preacher made his way to the podium, the door pushed open again and Chaz entered. She gestured to the empty spot beside her, and he tucked himself into it.

"Crowded tonight," he said.

"I guess everyone wants to count their blessings."

He smiled. "That's a good thing, I suppose."

The pastor welcomed everyone, and the room quieted. After a heartfelt prayer and some testimonies from the congregation, they sang "Count Your Blessings" and "We Gather Together to Ask the Lord's Blessing." The sound of Chaz' deep voice blending with her warm alto brought a smile to her lips.

The night's topic focused on gratitude and how it doesn't always happen naturally. Some things are harder to appreciate than others. Margie knew that to be the truth. It was hard to be grateful for all that had transpired with her husband, but she recognized the truth she found in God's word about all things working together for good for those who love God and are called according to His purpose. While she might not see that good in her earthly lifetime, she knew that in the end, her joy would be full.

After the service, Chaz stood and held out his hand to help her up. "Looking forward to the camping trip?"

"I am."

"Feel comfortable riding?"

"Still nervous but loving it."

"Good. Do you have plans for Thanksgiving dinner?"

"I'm planning to have dinner at the lodge." She smiled. "Then Casey and Gage are supposed to Skype if all goes well."

"That can be hit or miss, but I'm looking forward to talking to them tomorrow, too."

"Why don't we do it together?"

"Sure, but what would you say to dinner at my place instead of eating at the lodge? Carly and Thomas are coming down for Thanksgiving dinner."

"I don't want to disrupt your family time."

"Considering your daughter married my son, we are family now."

"True."

"So, would you care to come over for family dinner?"

"That sounds delightful. I'd love to."

~

THE AROMA OF TURKEY and stuffing filled the house, and Carly had set the round table with fine china she must've brought with her since he certainly hadn't packed any when he'd made the move.

As he was removing the biscuits from the oven, the doorbell rang. "That'll be Margie. I'll get it."

"I'm still shocked you invited her."

"Don't be. She's family."

"Ummhmm."

"Don't do that. We're just friends."

Carly followed him into the living room. "Sure, you are. What was it you said back when Casey and Gage were first seeing each other?" She giggled as he reached the front door. "That's right. 'Margie Crawford is a class act.'" Her impression of his voice was terrible, but the words were accurate.

He pulled the door open. "Come on in, Margie." Gesturing to Carly, he said, "You remember Carly."

"Of course, I do. Hi, Carly."

Carly gave her a brief hug. "It's good to see you. Have you heard from Casey and Gage?"

"Casey emailed this morning. They're supposed to Skype with us tonight."

"Us?" Carly gave them a knowing look and grinned.

Margie's cheeks reddened, and she cleared her throat. "I emailed Casey last night and told her I'd be having Thanksgiving dinner here."

A brief time later, they all settled around the table, and Thomas passed dishes piled high with turkey, stuffing, cranberry sauce, and more. After they'd all filled their plates, Carly lifted her eyes to Margie. "Dad mentioned that the two of you are going on a camping trip tomorrow."

"It's a Redemption Ranch event I happen to be attending that your father is working."

"So, it isn't a date?"

Chaz nearly choked on his water. "Carly!"

Thomas rubbed his forehead. "Hon. Not appropriate."

"I'm just curious."

"They're adults. Leave them be. I'm sure if, at some point, they become more than friends, you'll be invited to the wedding."

"Tommy boy, you're as bad as my daughter," Chaz said.

Margie finished chewing, and then joined the conversation. "I'm certain your father swore off women a long time ago. I've personally witnessed many eligible females make an attempt to take him off the market, but he's managed to elude their traps."

Chaz shook his head. "I think there is a football game on. I'll be in the living room." He hadn't watched a football game since all the kneeling nonsense started, but anything was better than sitting there listening to all their opinions on his love life or lack thereof.

CHAPTER 3

Friday morning, they set out on their adventure. A dark-haired young man named Levi was leading their group. He was respectful of the differing needs and skill levels of the riders. Levi set a moderate pace so beginners like her could keep up, but the more advanced riders weren't frustrated. Chaz brought up the rear. By mid-morning, Margie needed to stand in the stirrups occasionally to lift herself enough that she could readjust her position on Daisy. The horse was a dream, but she'd underestimated how sore she'd get after riding for a while. They had a long trek ahead of them, and she felt foolish for having believed she could handle it.

"You doing okay up there?" Chaz' voice came from behind her. She looked over her shoulder, but he rode up beside her since the trail had widened out enough to fit both of their horses.

"I'm fine." If you didn't count a sore bottom, a runny nose from the chilly air, and windburn.

"No need to lie. It's written all over your face."

"It's harder than I expected."

"Knew it would be, but you'll be all right. We're going to

stop in a bit for a picnic by Hidden Lake. I packed a couple of shock-absorbing saddle cushions in case any of the riders needed one. Should help you get through the remainder of the ride. And if you don't think you can make it back, you can catch a ride back on the truck that's bringing the food. It's meeting us for lunch and again near the camping spot."

Tears sprang to her eyes at his thoughtfulness, but she blinked them away. "Thank you."

Chaz sighed. "I was sorry the kids didn't manage to call last night."

"Me too. I was looking forward to talking to them."

"It's toughest on the holidays, isn't it?"

"It is. They're doing a wonderful thing over there, but I miss them something fierce." She stroked Daisy's long neck.

"Have you looked into the list of events they hold at the ranch? I think you'll enjoy quite a few of them."

She smiled. Chaz wasn't much of a talker, so he was clearly trying to keep her mind off her pain and the difficulty of the ride. It was kind of him. "I did. Your brother and sister-in-law really know how to show their guests a fun time."

∽

AFTER DISMOUNTING, CHAZ HELPED Margie do the same. He led their horses into their paddock then returned to where he'd left her. They walked to the cooler together, and he grabbed them each a bagged lunch and bottle of water.

"Shall we?" He gestured toward the lake where small groups were gathered eating their lunches. When they reached the shore, he spread a blanket and unpacked their meals.

"Thought you were cooking?"

"Sandwiches for lunch, but I will be making the evening meal. It's nothing fancy. Chili and skillet cornbread."

"Sounds delicious."

"Too bad Thomas and Carly couldn't stick around. Those two know how to cook."

"That chocolate mousse pie Thomas made was scrumptious. That girl of yours found herself the perfect husband. Nothing more attractive than a man who can cook."

Chaz raised an eyebrow. "That so?"

He watched as her cheeks turned a lovely shade of red as it dawned on her that she was talking to the man who was cooking for the entire group.

She tilted her face upward, soaking in the sunshine. "I thought it'd be colder this time of year."

"I'm surprised how nice it is. This is only my second time on this camping trip since they didn't start having it until after I'd moved away from Redemption. Last year it was chilly. You would've needed more than that thin jacket you call a coat."

"I'll be sore tomorrow, but I'm glad I did this."

Grinning, he leaned back on his elbows. "How are you liking ranch life?"

"It's everything I hoped it would be. I was looking for adventure, and I found it."

"Glad to hear it."

"I'm not sure it would've been as easy to fit in if I hadn't already known someone here. And Thanksgiving was nice at your place."

"We were happy to have you."

"Carly is a sweet kid. Not quite the same as the wild young woman she once was."

"I think that was mostly an act."

"Yeah. Casey went through one of those phases, too. The wild hair colors, crazy clothing, and odd music choices. Straight A's always, but she needed to make a statement that would separate her from her father. I think for a while that she forgot how to be herself."

"I'm glad she found her way. And that she and Gage found each other," Chaz said.

"Me too." She plucked a piece of grass and twirled it between her fingers.

~

As THE SUN SETTLED over the mountains in the distance, the group stopped at a clearing and set up tents while Chaz started a campfire. After she finished setting hers up, she took a seat on a log by the campfire and waited for dinner to be ready. She watched as Chaz reheated the chili he must've cooked ahead of time. Made sense since they stopped so late. He wouldn't have had time to properly cook the beans if he had waited.

After eating a bowl of chili with a definite kick to it,

Margie savored a piece of cornbread with honey butter. "This is good."

"I'm glad you like it. Chili too spicy for you?"

"Nah. I can take the heat, but the sweet cornbread is a nice contrast."

"You can take the heat, huh?"

She felt her face warm. The man knew how to throw her off balance with his teasing comments.

A young man with a guitar strummed a tune she recognized as Kumbaya. It was only a year earlier when her daughter explained to her that historians believed it was pidgin English and a transliteration for Come by here, Lord. Come by here. She couldn't know for sure if that was true, but she liked the thought, and hoped the Lord's presence would be felt around the campfire. Soon the rest of the group joined in, but Chaz remained silent until she elbowed him in the ribs. Then his rich bass joined the chorus.

When the song wound down, a young boy shouted. "Sing a Christmas song!"

"Which one?" the guitarist asked.

A sweet soprano broke the silence with the opening salvo for Silent Night and everyone listened quietly until the young woman asked them to join in for the second verse.

When the song ended, Chaz handed Margie a bag of marshmallows and a roasting stick, and she held a marshmallow over the fire until it caught then she blew out the flame.

"Intentional sabotage?"

"I like it burned."

"But the inside won't be soft and mushy."

She shrugged. He held out a Hershey bar and a pack of graham crackers. "Are you going to make it into a s'more or eat it like it is?"

"Both." She popped the burned marshmallow into her mouth and took another one to roast before passing the bag around. The woman to her left gave her a hard, cold stare, and she wondered what she'd done to offend her. "It's getting a bit chilly."

"Move closer to the fire." He stretched out his legs. "You ain't seen nothing yet. Wait another couple of hours. Hope you brought a warm sleeping bag."

"I'm from Freedom, you can't scare me with Colorado cold."

"We aren't nearly as cold down here as it is up on the ridge, but the frost does settle into the valley at night this time of year."

❧

WHEN THEY ARRIVED BACK at the barns late Saturday afternoon, Chaz dismounted and led his horse to the stable, glancing over his shoulder at Margie as he did. A ranch hand was helping her dismount. He should talk to her, but what would he say? The trip was successful, and they'd had a few good conversations, but he wasn't looking for complications. She lived in Freedom, and he'd made his home here now. She was still working as a real estate agent, and he was retired. Well, sort of. His brother liked keeping him busy, but he was quite sure it was more about giving him a purpose than an actual need for his services.

His life and Margie's life were too different. He was at least ten years older than her. Probably closer to fifteen. And there could be no crazier choice than to date his son's mother-in-law. If things went south, it would be all sorts of complicated.

No. The best thing to do was pretend the past twenty-four hours had never happened. Let her think he was simply being friendly or that he was some sort of player. As long as she didn't see the truth and realize his attraction for her was growing stronger every minute he spent in her presence.

He brushed down his horse and when he turned around, Leona was standing there with Goldenrod. She came alongside him, and they worked together to take care of the majestic animals. One of the ranch hands did the same for Daisy, Margie's mount, when she was brought into the stable. After all the horses were tended to, he said goodbye to Leona and headed back to his cabin. A few hours of mindless television was what he needed to get his head back on straight.

❦

MARGIE STRETCHED OUT HER sore muscles as she watched Chaz retreat into the barn. She wasn't sure what she'd expected from him. Maybe a few words or a suggestion for dinner together later, but she hadn't thought she'd be completely ignored. It was silly of her to think the trip meant more than it did. The spark she'd thought was igniting between them was in her imagination. He'd interacted with her the same way he would've with any other guest of the ranch.

She turned on the heel of her Lucchese boots and strode toward the lodge. Finding someone to dine with wouldn't be difficult.

When she entered the lobby, a crisp pine scent enveloped her. Connie was on a ladder placing a brilliant star on top of a massive Christmas tree. The sight reminded her of the reason for the season. She served a risen Savior, and He was a cause for celebration. The heaviness weighing her down lightened, and she grinned up at her hostess. "The star is gorgeous. Need any help?"

"I'm done here, but if you're serious about wanting to help, there is more decorating to be done elsewhere. We have to prepare for the annual barn dance."

"I'd love to help." And she meant it. Helping others was the best way to keep from dwelling on your own issues. Besides, she liked Connie. The woman seemed genuine and kind, so she hoped to get to know her better. Maybe they'd become friends. You could never have too many of those. She thought about Jan back home. They hadn't spent much time together lately. Jan was married now, and marriage changed everything.

"You should join me Monday morning then. I'm going to start with barn decorating, then bake a batch of cookies for ladies' Bible study. We'd love to have you join us."

"Are you sure I won't be intruding?"

"Nonsense. It'd be a joy to have you there."

CHAPTER 4

CHAZ WALKED TO THE Triple R Chapel for service. He'd decided against attending Redemption Bible in order to avoid running into Margie. The woman affected him, and he wasn't sure what to do about it yet. A pang of guilt shot through him. Service was about worship, so it shouldn't matter who else was present. The point was to praise the Lord and spend time in prayer.

He stepped inside and was struck once again by the beauty of the place. He found a seat near the back and nodded at a few friends. Many of the ranch staff chose to attend services here since it was right on the property. It was a bit more laid back than the Bible church, but both met his needs and gave him fellowship and time focused on his Creator.

When the pastor began his sermon about faith overcoming fear, Chaz listened closely as he expounded on the story of Abraham's fear over God asking him to offer Isaac on the altar. Then he went into the story of David when Saul was trying to kill him. Lastly, he spoke of Shadrach, Meshach, and Abednego and how they'd thrust aside their fears and trusted the Lord even to the point of being cast into a burning fiery furnace.

Chaz wanted that kind of faith. The type that fought through fear and faced hard things. After service, he made his way to the altar and took some time to get right with the Lord.

$$\sim$$

MARGIE FOLLOWED THE CROWD into the church hall. The pastor had insisted everyone was welcome to stay even if they hadn't brought a dish, but she felt awkward and uncomfortable attending the luncheon. Her eyes landed on the redhead from the camping trip. Leona. The death stare she gave her made her want to flee. Maybe she should.

Connie spotted her and waved her over. "Sit with us."

She smiled her thanks and took a seat. When it was their table's turn to fill their plates, she rose with everyone else and helped herself to a little of everything that looked appealing. When they returned to their seats, she glanced around at the other people sitting with them. She was fairly sure the younger couple were Barry and Connie's daughter and her husband, but she wasn't positive and didn't want to ask. "The food smells scrumptious."

"It always does." The young man pointed at a serving on her plate. "Connie made that green bean casserole. It's delicious."

She took a forkful. He was right. It was yummy.

"How was the horseback riding trip?" Barry asked.

"Painful." She laughed.

Connie cringed. "I was afraid of that."

"I'm glad I went, regardless. It was an experience I might never have had otherwise."

"Did my brother treat you well?" Barry raised an eyebrow.

She let out a laugh. "That's a loaded question, and I'm not touching it."

∽

ON MONDAY MORNING, CHAZ followed Barry into the barn. Decorating wasn't his thing. This was a task for his niece Cassie and her husband Jason. In fact, he'd heard a story about her almost falling off a ladder while decorating this barn last year. He glanced around. The young couple was nowhere to be found. Maybe they were on the rodeo circuit. The boy didn't have enough sense to keep his behind off a bull, but he couldn't say much since he'd participated in the sport in high school. The kid was good to Cassie, so Chaz liked him well enough.

His gaze landed on Margie who was stringing up lights with Connie. He should probably apologize for being an idiot the last time he'd seen her, but something kept his feet cemented in place.

"Things progressing with the blonde divorcée?"

"Don't call her that. She has a name."

"Well?"

"What is it I'm supposed to be doing?"

"Asking the woman out."

"I meant what do you want me to do in here?"

"You and I are going to hang glitter-encrusted snowflakes from the ceiling."

"You're kidding?"

"I kid you not." Barry gave him a box of snowflakes and string then handed him a stapler. "Grab a ladder and get to work."

He chatted with his nephews, Zeke and Gideon, who were both recruited to help decorate, as well. About an hour and fifty snowflakes in, he caught sight of Margie leaving with Connie. No goodbye or anything. Not that he deserved one after the way he'd ignored her following the trip, but he didn't think she was the petty sort who would hold it against him. Drawing in a lungful of air, he descended the ladder. Maybe he'd go see what the women were up to.

～

MARGIE TOOK THE APRON Connie handed her, pulled it over her head, tied it, then laughed at the "kiss the cook" slogan across the front of it. She set to work measuring the ingredients Connie lined up on the counter beside the recipe card.

"Now that we're alone, tell me more about the camping trip?"

"It was physically demanding and emotionally draining."

"Care to elaborate? I expected the first part, but not the

second. What made it emotional?"

"Chaz Buchanan."

"My brother-in-law. Interesting! I knew you two were acquainted, but is there something going on between you?"

"I don't know. Probably not." She frowned.

"Knock, knock." It was Chaz. Margie didn't need to look up when she heard his voice.

"What can we do for you, Chaz?"

"Came by to talk with Margie."

Connie grinned and looked at each of them in turn. "I'll leave you to it." And before Margie knew what was happening, her new friend had ditched her.

"What are you up to?" he asked.

"Baking cookies."

"You left the barn in a hurry."

"Umm hmm."

"Did I do something to offend you?"

"Not at all. Why would you think that?"

He frowned and scrubbed a hand over his face. "Maybe it's my imagination, but it feels like you're avoiding me."

"Am I?"

Chaz let out a deep sigh. "Margie, I know I rushed off when we returned to the barn."

She stirred the mixture in the bowl with more force than necessary. "You don't have to explain yourself to me."

"Then what is this?"

"It was clear I was reading too much into your kindness, so I backed off."

He leaned against the kitchen island, and his eyes bored into hers. "Knock it off."

"Knock what off?"

"The silent treatment. Then pretending nothing is wrong. We're adults here, there is no reason to play games."

"I'm not playing games, Mr. Buchanan."

"I asked you to call me Chaz."

"Seems to me you should reserve that privilege for your friends the same way you did back in Freedom."

"Our kids are married."

She kept her gaze trained on him, refusing to give him the satisfaction of looking away from his intense stare. "Is that why you were being nice to me. For Casey?"

"Stop it."

"Stop what." She stuck out her bottom lip.

His gaze moved to her lips, and he placed his hands on her shoulders. She was surprised at the gentleness in his touch. The harshness of his words left her expecting something else entirely. "You probably shouldn't wear an apron with a blatant invitation on it unless you mean it."

"Maybe I do."

He leaned in closer and brushed the hair off her face. "Maybe I want to find out for sure."

"Ya'll seen Connie around?" Barry's booming voice carried through the room, causing her to jump.

"I'm sure she didn't go far. She'll be back in a minute." Margie couldn't stop the words from flowing. She felt like she'd been caught doing something wrong. She and Chaz were adults. If they'd been about to share a kiss, there was nothing wrong with that. "We're baking cookies for the women's Bible study. Chocolate chip cookies and snickerdoodles topped with taffy bits."

"Yum." Barry looked from her to Chaz and then back again. "Did I interrupt something?"

"No," Margie and Chaz answered simultaneously.

"Nothing to see here, right." Barry chuckled. "Tell my wife to save me some of those cookies."

❧

CHAZ PUSHED OPEN HIS front door with more force than necessary. Margie had him all tangled up. One minute he was as agitated as a bull trying to throw his rider, and the next moment he was ready to cuddle kittens. The woman had him turned all inside out and upside down.

If he was going to sort any of this out, he needed food. He snatched the deli meat and a jar of Hellman's from his fridge, then grabbed a loaf of bread. Once his sandwich was ready, he sat on a stool at the counter and dug in. When they'd been on the camping trip, Margie had squirted mustard on her ham and cheese then added potato chips to her sandwich. She said the crunch gave it something special. He'd have to try it that way sometime.

The woman claimed she wasn't playing games, but if that was true, why the cold shoulder? And then there was that moment between them in the kitchen. Her eyes shone with a mixture of confusion, attraction, and challenge. She'd been daring him to kiss her. He would've, too. If Barry hadn't chosen that moment to interrupt them, as sure as he had breath in his lungs, he would've accepted that woman's challenge.

She was aggravating. Talked too much. There was nothing about her that was even remotely similar to his meek and mild wife, Suzanne. God rest her soul. She'd been quiet and domestic. Content to stay home and raise babies. Margie spent her life working to make a name for herself in real estate. And she'd done it, too. Everyone knew who to see if they wanted to make a purchase or find someone to look over rental properties in Freedom, Colorado.

Too bad she'd had a no-good ex-husband. Chaz had seen the damage John's actions had done to his daughter. And his wife, when she'd been kidnapped by the father of one of John's victims as a means of revenge. Thankfully, most people realized Margie and Casey had nothing at all to do with his crimes, and they embraced them both as part of the community. But she'd never remarried, and now it seemed she'd set her sights on him. Casey had mentioned her mother's interest, but he'd blown off the comment. It was hard to ignore Margie when she was here in Redemption and hanging out with his sister-in-law.

He would talk the whole thing through with his brother if he didn't think it would bring on merciless teasing. Besides, he knew what Barry would say. He'd tell him to go for it. He'd been a widower far longer than he was married, and it was time to move on. To let Suzanne go and learn to love someone new. It was something he'd never seriously considered. Until now.

CHAPTER 5

WHEN THEY ARRIVED IN the fellowship hall of Redemption Bible Church, Connie set down the tray of brownies next to the coffee urn before handing Margie a mug and a paper plate. "Let's get our goodies and take our seats."

She did as Connie suggested and sat, then took a sip of the strong brew. The chairs were set up in a circle like they were children about to play duck, duck, goose or musical chairs. An awkward silence came over the room as everyone studied the newcomer, but Connie eased it with a brief introduction.

"Margie came along with me. She's a real estate agent in Freedom. I'm sure you've heard of it."

A woman with a blue streak in her short white hair smiled. "I've been there. Stayed at Freedom Ridge Resort. Why would you ever leave?"

Connie smiled. "Pearl, maybe you've forgotten that Redemption is beautiful, too."

Pearl tapped fingernails painted a bright blue on her notebook. "If you like ranches. Sure."

"And spectacular sunrises and sunsets," Margie said. "This area is every bit as breathtaking as Freedom. It's different, but just as amazing."

Connie opened her Bible. "Margie is here for vacation. She wanted an adventure."

"Are you finding one?"

"I sure am."

"Let's turn in our Bibles to Philippians chapter two, verse four." Connie read aloud. "Look not every man on his own things, but every man also on the things of others."

"If you've been following our study guide, you probably have some thoughts on the verse. Shall we go around and share?"

Desiree, the young lady to Connie's right, was the first to share. She glanced at her notebook before raising her eyes to the group. "Before I took the time to apply the verse to my life, I would get annoyed when my mom couldn't babysit for me. I thought she was being unreasonable. But after applying it, I realize I need to take into consideration what my mother might be going through that I don't even know about."

Margie considered her words. She couldn't be more than twenty-two, but there was wisdom in her speech. She'd been doing the same thing with Chaz. Failing to consider what he might be going through or why he might've needed to take a step back and distance himself when they returned from the camping trip.

Pearl shared next. "It's easy to get caught up in our own daily struggles. So much so that we forget to look around and see the suffering of others. I think that is one of the best things about keeping a prayer journal. It reminds me to consider others and the needs they face. Our God is mighty and will work wonders if we only take the time to ask."

"Yes, Pearl. That's absolutely right. While God may not always answer in the way we think is best, He knows the end from the beginning, and His will is always perfect." Connie smiled. "Did you want to share, Margie?"

"I was struck by Desiree's words. I've been so focused on my own feelings about a situation, that I've neglected to consider someone else's. This was a much-needed wakeup call for me."

"And for the rest of us, I hope." Connie closed her Bible.

～

WHEN QUITTING TIME CAME around, Chaz headed back to his cabin. Staring into his freezer, he frowned at the slim selection of microwave meals looking back at him. Nothing appealed. Eating at the lodge was an option, but he'd probably run into Margie, and she'd want an explanation for whatever it was that possessed him to come so close to kissing her earlier. Wouldn't surprise him if she demanded to know his intentions and whether he wanted to pursue her or if he was, as he'd accused her of doing, playing games.

Heaven help him, he wasn't sure he had answers for any of those questions or the myriad others he was sure the woman would come up with. She was never short of words, but he stammered over his. In the business world, he'd been fierce. He gave instructions. Some would claim he barked out orders, but was there a difference, really? A smile touched his lips. Yes. There was. His daughter had proven that. She was a force to be reckoned with, but she treated everyone with kindness. He didn't have her gentle demeanor though. And he certainly couldn't start ordering Margie around. The way he'd grilled her at the Reynolds' residence was bad enough. If he wanted more to develop between them, he needed to watch his tongue. But was that what he wanted?

Closing the freezer door, he made a decision. Dinner out. A meal at Flapjacks was the perfect solution to fill his empty stomach without running into the woman who made him think about things he hadn't considered since Suzanne died.

Thirty minutes later, he pushed through the door into Flapjacks and took a seat in an empty booth. The aroma of burnt coffee and fried food was familiar and comforting. Agnes hustled over to his table.

"Evening, Chaz. The specials tonight are chicken fried steak or trout and chips. What's your pleasure?"

"I'll go with the trout and glass of unsweetened tea."

"Coming right up." She retreated into the back, and he looked around the diner. Not many people out and about, but it was early. It might get crowded later when people finished their Christmas shopping. He lifted the plastic display from the table and inspected the desserts before turning it over. An advertisement for a book signing. And it was taking place now. He wasn't much for fawning over celebrities, but it was an author whose writing he enjoyed. Maybe he'd stop over. If it wasn't too crowded, he might even get a book signed. His son-in-law, Thomas, read Ethan Thorn's political thrillers, too. He could purchase a copy and get it autographed for him for Christmas.

Agnes returned to his table with a glass of mostly ice with some tea in it. In two sips it was gone. He should've asked her to go easy on the ice. When she delivered his meal, she noticed it was empty and brought over the pitcher to fill his glass.

"You hear anything about this book signing?" Chaz asked.

"I sure have. Half the town claims they'll be attending. Probably why it's dead in here tonight. Everyone wants to support Bethany. That poor woman has had a rough go of it. Relocated here over the summer. The sadness in her eyes is unmistakable. Wish there was more we could do for her."

He wondered what Bethany had been through but didn't ask the question. No reason to encourage Agnes' propensity for gossip. "Maybe I'll stop by there when I finish my meal."

When Agnes left his table, he dug into his food. The flaky texture of the fish contrasted nicely with the crunch from the deep-fried batter coating it. He couldn't eat like this every night, but it was a nice change. The thick natural-cut french fries were perfectly seasoned and hit the spot.

～

MARGIE PULLED UP OUTSIDE of the bookshop. On their way back from Bible study, Connie had told her about the restored barn that had been converted into a bookstore. As much as she was missing Stories & Scones and her good friend Jan, she thought visiting the local bookstore might make her feel more at home while she was here in Redemption. She pushed open the rustic wooden door leading into Bethany's Book Barn. When she finally got it to budge, she stepped inside and was immediately captivated by the space. Red steel farmhouse-style lights hung from the wooden beams. Shelves filled with books took up half the first floor and from what she could tell, most of the loft. There were seats scattered around where customers could relax with a book.

To her left, she noticed patrons seated around tables made from repurposed spools decorated with red lanterns. She ordered a mocha latte and took a seat at an empty table. The glow coming from the lanterns proved to be of the battery-operated variety, but it didn't lessen the ambiance.

A hush fell over everyone when famed author Ethan Thorn came out from behind a curtain onto a small platform beside a display table filled with his books. She smiled. His eyes locked with hers, and he hopped down from the platform to greet her.

"Margie. It's been a long time."

"It has. How are you?"

"Career is fabulous."

"But how are you?"

"I've been better. This book tour is wearying."

Margie took a long sip of mocha-flavored goodness. "I'll bet."

"What are you doing in Redemption?"

"Vacationing at Redemption Ranch. Casey married a missionary and moved to Bangladesh, so I needed an adventure of my own."

"Wow. Bangladesh?"

"Wasn't what I expected for her, but she's happy."

"Good. She was a good kid."

"She's not a kid anymore."

"No. I guess not." His eyes searched hers. "I haven't seen you since..."

"Since John went to prison."

"Right."

"I heard you were going to be here tonight, so I thought I'd stop in and say hello."

"I'm glad you did." He pointed behind him with his thumb. "Can we catch up after? I have to do this thing."

"That'd be nice."

~

THE MOMENT CHAZ BUSTLED into Bethany's Book Barn, the rich scent of expensive coffee hit him. He might as well be back in Freedom Ridge at the Mountain Mug or Stories and Scones. He glanced at his watch. If he had a cup now, he'd be up all night, but who could resist a rich Italian espresso? He sidled up to the counter and ordered one then scanned the room while he waited for it. His eyes rested on Margie. He hadn't expected to see her there. Wait. Was she talking with Ethan Thorn? She was, and there was a sense of familiarity between them. It was disconcerting. Could she have a thing going with the famous author?

He sucked in a ragged breath and reached for his tiny

cup. The envy raging through him was new, and he didn't like it. It was more than the discomfort he'd felt when Margie took lessons from Paul. Downing what remained of his drink, he gathered his courage then strode to Margie's table.

Her smile was warm and welcoming as she gestured to the seat beside hers. "This is an unexpected surprise. Have a seat. I think Ethan is going to do a reading before they start the signing."

"Ethan? On a first name basis with one of the top thriller writers in the country?"

She waved off his question. "Ethan Thornton is an old friend through my ex-husband."

"Thornton?"

"Thorn is a pen name."

"Ah." He smiled. "Thought maybe the two of you were more than friends."

Her throaty laugh filled the air. "Never considered it a possibility. He's a great guy but having met through John and becoming friends with his wife before she became his ex ... it would be super-duper weird."

"Oh. Makes sense."

"What brings you to Ethan's signing? Are you a fan?"

"I enjoy his books, but I'm here to get a book signed for Thomas. Thought it would make a good Christmas gift."

"That's thoughtful." She plucked a piece of glitter from the collar of his shirt. "Dabbling in glitter art?"

"Even after my shower I'm finding glitter everywhere. I blame Connie and those snowflakes of hers."

She let out a giggle. "The silver glitter is a nice contrast to your eyes."

Chaz frowned and shook his head.

"I'm going to grab a hot tea. Can I get you anything?" Margie asked as she stood.

"Let me get it for you."

"No. Really. I need to stretch my legs. I'm still sore from horseback riding."

"Okay. I could use a bottle of water if you're sure you don't mind." He fished a few bills from his pocket, but she refused them.

CHAPTER 6

By the time Wednesday morning rolled around, Margie was trying hard to keep up the charade of the happy-go-lucky single vacationer and failing. Breathing in a sharp breath, she turned her attention to the scenery outside her window. The morning had been spent alternating between staring outside and scrolling through her Facebook notifications. Though she'd considered deleting the app, it allowed her brief updates into the lives of old friends she wouldn't normally hear from, so she'd chosen to keep it. Friends like Cecilia Thornton. Ethan's ex-wife. She'd been among the few people who had stuck around after John's arrest. That time in her life was one of the deepest valleys she'd been through, and going through it alone so much of the time made it even harder. Casey had withdrawn into herself, and most of her former acquaintances avoided her for months after the news broke. She realized later it was because they didn't have words to express their empathy, but she wished they'd had the courage to try. Their silent presence would've been better than their complete absence.

Her laptop dinged an alert, so she moved her mouse to bring the screen to life. It was a video call from Casey, so she clicked to accept.

"Hi, sweetheart."

"Hey, Mom. How was your Thanksgiving? Are you enjoying your time at the ranch?"

"It was lovely, and yes, I am."

"Gage hasn't been able to get a hold of his dad, do you know if he's around?"

"I think I saw him downstairs. If you want, I can take my laptop down there and see if he's still there."

"That'd be great." Margie unplugged her computer and headed down the stairs. When she reached the bottom, she stumbled over the area rug, and a warm hand reached out to steady her.

"Probably not a good idea to descend stairs while staring at your computer," Chaz grumbled.

"I found your father-in-law. He kept me from doing a face plant, but he's a bit grouchy about it."

Chaz raised an eyebrow.

"I have Casey on the line. She said Gage was having trouble reaching you."

"I'm not great at keeping up with stuff on my computer."

"I imagine he tried your cell, too."

"Most times I keep the volume off." He gestured for her to go ahead of him. "Let's grab a seat."

She followed behind as he led the way to a cozy seating area with two couches and a chair around a fireplace. After setting the laptop on the table, she scooted closer to Chaz and pulled one of the geometric-patterned pillows into her lap, hugging it close while she bit her lip and awaited her daughter's news.

"So, why have you been trying to reach me?" Chaz asked.

Casey adjusted the screen so they could see Gage beside her in the cafe she knew was more than an hour from the village where they lived. "We have some news."

"What's that?" Margie asked. She hoped they were planning to return home. Her heart ached knowing Casey was so far from home and that she was in constant danger.

"We're going to have a baby. I'm pregnant."

Margie drew in a sharp breath and the world spun around her. She was going to be a grandmother, but her grandchild would be born on the other side of the world.

Chaz' booming voice interrupted her thoughts. "That's wonderful news. Congratulations to you both."

"I know it's not ideal for us to start a family while we're here, but we're ready for whatever God has in store for us." Gage threaded his fingers together with Casey's.

Right. God. That's what she needed to remember. God was in control, and if it was His will for them to start a family in Bangladesh, then she would support them.

Chaz put an arm around her shoulders and gave her a squeeze. "We're both so happy for you."

"Yes." Margie pasted on a smile. "I'm looking forward to being called Nanna. Can't wait for you guys to visit home."

"Won't be too much longer." Casey smiled. "We're hoping to take a furlough shortly after the baby is born."

"I'll be praying for all three of you in the meantime," Margie said.

❧

As Chaz made the turn, he waved to Leona who was exiting the hidden drive that led to his brother's house. She was making herself at home on the ranch. He saw her riding that horse all over the place. It was nice to see her getting the most out of her time there. But right now, he was looking forward to a home-cooked meal. Since he left Freedom, he rarely had one. It wasn't that Barry and Connie didn't invite him. He had a standing invitation. And his sister-in-law reiterated it often. He simply didn't want to intrude. Tonight was different. They would want to hear the good news.

Connie met him at the door, and he followed her inside. After a few minutes of greetings, they all took their seats around the dining room table and Zeke brought out the food.

"Looks good and smells better."

"Thanks. I think," Zeke said.

Gideon leaned back in his chair, stretching his long legs out in front of him. "How's ranch life treating you, Uncle Chaz?"

"Last few days, it's making me think I should go back to the business world. Your dad doesn't give me any time off."

"Not true. You can work as much or as little as you want, and you know it." Barry frowned.

"Maybe. But the inventories have been off lately, so I've been working twice as hard to get it sorted out."

"That's probably my fault. I'm terrible about signing

things out." Gideon shrugged. "I'm not used to having someone around checking it."

"Get better at it. Please." Chaz laughed. "Your sister wants this place run like a well-oiled machine."

"She would." Gideon wrapped his knuckles on the table. "We gonna pray so we can eat?"

Barry asked the Lord's blessing, and they all dug into the beef Wellington, garlic mashed potatoes and steamed asparagus. "This food is delicious."

Zeke grinned. "I've been experimenting."

"He's addicted to the Food Network," Gideon said.

"I have some news." Chaz looked around the table. "Barry and Connie, you're going to be a great-aunt and great-uncle."

"Is Carly expecting?" Connie asked.

"Not that I'm aware of, but Casey is," Chaz said.

"Really? She's going to have a baby. Over there?" Barry asked.

Chaz nodded. "Yes. God's protection has surrounded them since they took this assignment, and their ministry has been fruitful. I don't think they have plans to leave the missionary field, but they are planning a furlough shortly after the baby is born."

"That's wonderful news. A new baby, and we get to see them soon." Connie smiled.

"Yes, it is. It's a big step for them, but a good one," Chaz said.

"You're gonna be a grandfather. That means you're old," Barry said.

"I knew I was old before getting this news." He chuckled.

~

EARLY FRIDAY MORNING, MARGIE shuffled from one foot to the other trying to keep warm as she waited with the rest of the group of vacationers eagerly awaiting the start of their guided hike. The brochure in her room said it offered stunning views of Colorado's red rock canyons, and she was looking forward to this next leg of her adventure. It promised to be an amazing day.

A thin layer of snow covered the area, making it feel like a winter wonderland. She looped her scarf around her neck to fight the chill. Her breath was visible in the crisp, chilly air, but it was December, so she'd expected as much. She'd warm up once they got moving.

"For those of you who don't know me yet, I'm Gideon. If you forget that, just shout 'hey you,' and I'll answer." He grabbed his backpack, and they all fell in step behind him. "There may be icy patches this morning, so please watch where you're walking. We wouldn't want any accidents."

About ten minutes into their walk, the roar of the Dolores River's rushing waters reached them. The snow-dusted mountains against the azure sky offered a striking contrast, and she snapped some photos with her cell phone.

When they finally arrived at the overlook an hour into the hike, she stood on the platform and admired the view of the river far below. She leaned against the rail and bowed her head, offering praise and thanksgiving for the majesty surrounding them. God's artistry never ceased to amaze her. Looking up, she realized she was alone, and hurried to rejoin her group.

As she stepped off the platform, her foot slipped on a patch of ice hidden beneath the snow. Her heart leapt as she slid down the slope and off the trail. After rolling a few times, she managed to grab onto some brush and steady herself.

"Are you okay down there?" a male voice called out.

"I think so." She waited until her breathing steadied and then attempted to climb back up the slope, but a sharp, stabbing pain in her knee stopped her.

"Margie?"

"Something's wrong with my knee."

~

CHAZ SAT OPPOSITE BARRY in the office. He'd brought him the latest inventory numbers. They were going down every week. Enough that it was concerning him. His brother looked at his phone. "Looks like there was an accident on the morning hike. Gideon says Margie took a fall."

"Is it serious?"

"Doesn't sound like it, but he doesn't think she can make the trek back on her own without assistance. He's going to help her but needs someone else to meet them to lead the rest of the group on the return trip."

"I'll go. Gideon can stay with the hikers, and I'll get Margie with Daisy. She's a sturdy mount that can hold the two of us with no trouble."

"That'll work. I'll text Gideon and tell him you're on your way."

Chaz hurried to the barn and saddled Daisy. He moved over the tricky, but familiar terrain with relative ease, but his thoughts kept drifting to Margie and how badly she might've been hurt. Barry said it wasn't serious, but what if he was wrong? His own medical emergency a couple of years earlier left him cognizant that things weren't always as they seemed.

When he finally arrived, the relieved expression on Margie's face made the ride well worth the effort. "How about a ride with Daisy and me?"

"I'd appreciate that, Chaz. Thanks for coming."

He helped her onto the horse and tipped his hat to Gideon before heading back down the trail toward the lodge.

CHAPTER 7

Margie winced when her foot hit the stirrup as Chaz helped her dismount. He handed the reins off to a stable boy then turned back to her.

"You okay?"

She smiled through the pain. "I'll be fine."

"We should probably take you for x-rays."

"No. I'm sure it isn't anything too serious. I'd rather avoid the hospital if possible."

He frowned. "Doesn't seem like the wise choice."

"Tell you what, if it isn't any better by tomorrow morning, I'll go have it checked out."

"Okay." He wound his arm around her back. "Lean on me, and I'll help you back to your room."

Once she was settled on the loveseat in her room, he stood awkwardly in the doorway. "Have a seat, Chaz. Unless you have to hurry back to work?"

He chuckled and took a seat on the chair beside her. "I make my own hours. I'm supposed to be retired, remember?"

"You sure don't act like someone who has retired."

"I blame my brother." He smiled. "He and Connie were

53

worried about me out in Freedom with Gage gone and Carly married. They convinced me to come and help them out. Turned out they didn't really need my assistance but wanted to convince me to come and knew their deception would work."

"Seems it worked like a charm."

"Sure did."

"Do you regret moving out here?"

"I don't." He stretched his legs out in front of him. "I miss being closer to Carly, but we probably see each other nearly as often as we would if I was still in Freedom."

"What about work? Do you miss that?"

"Once in a while, but I don't miss the daily grind. I only miss certain aspects of the work."

"That's good. I can understand why you stayed here. It's been lonely in Freedom since Casey left."

"What about your friends? You have book club with Jan and those realtor friends of yours."

"I'm the only single woman. Divorced. Makes me feel like there's something wrong with me."

"Nonsense. Your divorce wasn't your fault. Nobody blames you for escaping that marriage."

"He actually served me with the divorce papers."

"From prison?"

"Yeah."

"Wow. I never would've guessed that. The man goes away for rape and serves his wife with divorce papers. That's a new low."

"It was a blessing. I'm not sure I would've had the courage to divorce him and cause even more ripples in

Casey's life, but he took the decision out of my hands."

"Maybe God's hand was in it."

"Yeah. Maybe." She sighed. "What God joined together let no man put asunder, right?"

"Jesus said fornication was a legitimate reason to seek divorce. I'm pretty sure your divorce qualified for that exemption."

"Yeah, I know. I just never thought I'd wind up divorced and alone."

"Has he bothered you since he got out of prison?"

"No. Haven't heard from him. He went to see Casey though."

"How did that go?"

"I think she got the closure she needed."

They talked for another hour about lighter topics before Chaz stood. "I guess I should go, I need to run to the feed store."

"Thanks for coming to my rescue."

❧

LATER THAT AFTERNOON, CHAZ picked up his pace and rubbed his hands together to warm them. The day was turning blustery. He suspected the inventory sheets would be sitting right where he'd left them. As he walked past the barn, someone scooted out the back with a box on his shoulder. He called out, but the young man didn't answer. Strange.

As the kid turned to leave through the back door, he was

able to see his profile, but he didn't look familiar.

Barry stepped out of the office as he approached the door. "Wasn't expecting you back today."

"Left the inventory sheets inside. I need to run in and grab them." He hurried in and snatched the pages then caught back up with his brother as he was opening the door to his truck. "Did you hire a new teenager to help in the barn?"

"No. There's no new young people on staff."

"That's funny. Just saw a kid I didn't recognize carrying a box out of the barn. Didn't stop when I called out to him."

"You're sure it wasn't one of our regulars?"

"Positive."

"I guess it could be a guest helping themselves to things. Maybe we need security to put cameras up in the tack room."

"Sounds like an excellent plan. I'm headed to Crescent Feed and Supply. Need me to pick up anything that is not on this list?"

"I could join you and after we could go into town and do some Christmas shopping."

"Shopping? You want me to go shopping?"

"I'm guessing you haven't gotten anything for Carly, and you're probably going to want to get Margie something. The two of you have been growing close lately."

He probably should get Margie a gift, but was it too forward of him to buy her a Christmas present? After such a long time out of the game, he didn't know how to play anymore.

∽

THE AROMA OF BEEF stew reached her as Margie left her room, intent on grabbing something to eat. She'd been planning to go into town, but she followed her nose into the dining area. Guests were scattered about, and the Callaways, a retired couple from Texas, waved her over. She sat with them along with a young travel writer from New York named Leticia.

"Is your ankle better?" Betsy asked.

Margie grimaced. "It was actually my knee I hurt. I'm well enough to move around, but it aches something fierce."

Leticia frowned. "Sounds painful."

"It is, but I'll be okay." Intent on changing the conversation, she asked, "How are you enjoying Colorado?"

"Loving it so far. I can't wait to write this spread for our magazine. The pictures are going to be phenomenal." Leticia's eyes lit with excitement.

"I'll bet." Margie smiled. "Did you get some from the overlook?"

"My photographer did. He sent me his photos, and they're absolutely perfect."

"Can't wait to read the article."

"You'll have to wait until next month." She grinned. "I think you're the only one staying here who's actually from Colorado. Is it different here than it is where you're from?"

"Sure is. Freedom gets its name from Freedom Ridge

which is where the ski resort is located. We get quite a bit more snow up there than you'll find in the lower elevations. The beauty is entirely different. The red rock you see everywhere down here isn't quite so prevalent as you ascend into the mountains."

They chatted as they ate, and Margie enjoyed the camaraderie. She'd needed it, but by the time dessert was served she was ready to scoot out, so she grabbed a bowl of apple crisp and headed into the living area where she took a seat in the same spot she'd sat in when taking the call from Casey informing her she was going to be a grandmother. After savoring a few bites of apple flavored with cinnamon and vanilla, she punched in Jan's number. She could use a taste of home right about now.

~

BARRY PARKED HIS PICKUP at a parking meter along the curb. The meters were covered with decorative bags, giving residents and visitors a break from parking fees during the busy holiday season. Chaz climbed out and closed his door, then faced the row of stores all decked out in festive adornments.

The scene was like something out of a Hallmark movie. All they needed was a girl inheriting a bakery and a rich city guy willing to give it all up to be with her. The fact that he'd seen too many of those movies was not something he was proud of, but when your daughter loses her mom young, you do what you have to do. So, he'd been the one to watch cheesy movies and drink hot chocolate with her.

His brother groaned beside him. "I'm not looking forward to this."

"It was your idea."

"What was I thinking?"

"That you can't wake up Christmas morning without a gift for your wife?"

"Yep. That was it."

"Want to try that place?" Chaz pointed to the sign for Olive and Sage. "Connie likes to cook. They might have something in there she'll like."

"Sure. Why not?"

They stared at the shelves of artfully arranged jars and bottles of spices. "I don't know what I'm doing."

The proprietor asked a few questions about Connie's cooking style and suggested a bottle of lavender-infused olive oil. Barry purchased it and they moved on to the next place.

Bells jangled as they entered a clothing store. A young woman hurried over. "May I help you find anything?"

"I'm looking for a Christmas gift for my son's mother-in-law."

The woman raised an eyebrow.

Barry chimed in. "He's in a new relationship with this woman. They've known each other for years, but they're starting to date."

"We're not dating." Chaz felt his face flush. "We're just friends."

"Sure you are."

The woman smiled knowingly. "I have the perfect

thing." She led him to a table of scarves. "These are elegant and stylish, so it'll look like you put some thought into the gift, but it won't be an over-the-top this-is-too-much-too-soon thing like jewelry."

"Sounds good." He rifled through the scarves until he found one in a lovely cream color he thought she'd appreciate. "This one will do."

She rang them up and they moved on to the next store.

Barry shrugged his shoulder. "What are you going to get Carly?"

"I'll probably go back to that cooking oil place."

"Olive and Sage?"

"Yeah. I should've gotten her something while we were there."

"Let's head back."

CHAPTER 8

On Saturday morning, Margie held the rail as she made her way downstairs. Yesterday's fall left her muscles sore in places she didn't even know she had them. Her knee felt better, but she was favoring her left leg since she was afraid to put too much weight on the right one.

The front door opened and Chaz waltzed in as she neared the bottom of the staircase.

"Good morning, Margie. Should you be coming down without any help?"

She chuckled. "I'm fine. No real damage except to my ego."

Chaz hurried to her and offered his arm. "Where are you headed?"

"To the living area."

He helped her settle into her favorite seat, and he placed a pillow on the table so she could keep her foot elevated. Instead of complying, she tucked her feet up under her. "I'm okay. No need to fuss."

"You're sure?" He frowned. "I was going to take you to urgent care to get checked out if it wasn't any better."

"Is that why you're here? To check in on me?"

He nodded and sank into the seat beside her.

Something outside the window caught her attention, and she watched as a teenager she'd seen behind the counter at Bethany's Book Barn the previous week made some sort of exchange with another young man in a manner that looked a lot like a drug deal. She shook her head. There was no reason to believe such a thing. For all she knew he'd purchased a Christmas gift for the other guy, and they were exchanging money for that. Her suspicious nature made everyone seem suspect.

"What are you watching out there?"

"Nothing. Just a couple of kids." No reason to cast aspersions on them over what might be an innocent exchange.

"Well, if you're better, what are your plans for the day?"

"I offered to help set up for the Noel Navigators event, but I want to rest my knee, so I can go to the Christmas barn dance."

He cleared his throat. "That was the other thing I was wondering about. How would you feel about accompanying me there tonight?"

She searched his eyes, trying to decipher his intent. "You mean like a date?"

He grinned. "Not *like* a date. An honest-to-goodness date."

"I'd like that."

"Good. Pick you up at seven?"

"I'll be here."

"Now, I'd better go help set up for the geo-cache event."

"If I'd known you were going to be there, I might not

have bailed out."

"It's best you rest so you'll be ready to two-step tonight."

"Thanks for coming by to check on me."

He nodded and headed for the door.

∾

CASSIE SAT IN THE passenger seat beside Chaz as he headed away from the Reynolds' residence.

"Where do you want to hide the first treasure?" he asked.

"How about over by the Triple R Chapel?" She held up a snow-globe ornament with a church scene inside it.

"Perfect." He parked the truck, and they walked the remainder of the way.

Cassie wrapped the item in tissue paper and placed it in one of the small wooden boxes engraved with *Noel Navigators* that they'd had made for the event. Connie thought they would double nicely as keepsake boxes for the guests.

They found a good spot by the base of the gazebo and tucked the treasure in between two rocks. She stood and brushed her hands on her jeans. "What do you think?"

"I'm wondering what you even need me here for?"

She laughed. "I might need you to lift some heavy rocks."

"In that case, you might've been better off bringing your husband along. This old man doesn't have the strength he used to."

"I don't believe that for a minute, Uncle Chaz."

"Where to next?"

"How about over by the spa?"

"Sure thing."

When they reached the spa, she hid the next item—a miniature nativity scene—behind some stones that circled one of the raised fireplaces.

When they were finished, it was nearing time for him to shower and change for the barn dance.

~

MARGIE DRESSED IN A black western-style skirt and paired it with a red blouse to make it more festive. She was downstairs sitting by the fire when Chaz arrived five minutes earlier than expected.

"You're ready early?"

"Real estate agents learn to be on time or risk dealing with annoyed clients."

He nodded his understanding. "Shall we?" He took her coat from the back of the couch and held it out so she could slip her arms in. Then he offered his arm, and she took hold. "You look amazing, by the way."

"Thank you." She smiled. "You don't look so bad yourself. Love the cowboy hat. It suits you."

They pulled up in a parking area already overflowing with vehicles. Chaz came around to the passenger side to help her out.

"Thanks."

A smile lit his eyes. "Did I mention I love a woman in cowgirl boots?"

She couldn't hold back a laugh. "No. I don't believe you

did." She was glad she wore them. At the last minute, her concerns over her knee had her ditching her three-inch heels and changing into the boots to avoid further injury.

When they entered the barn, they were ensconced in a winter wonderland. The glittery snowflakes glowed under the twinkling lights. The space hadn't looked nearly as ethereal in the daylight when they'd been hanging the decorations. She felt like they'd been transported to another place and time.

"Let me grab you a mug of Connie's Cowboy Christmas Cider. You're going to love it."

"What makes you think I haven't already tried it?"

"She only makes it once a year for the Christmas barn dance, and since this is your first time attending, I'm fairly certain you haven't had the pleasure."

While Chaz went to get her drink, she made small talk with Leticia, the travel writer she'd had dinner with the previous night.

"How's the knee?" Leticia asked.

"Better." She smiled. "It was sore enough to keep me from wearing high heels though."

"I'll bet."

"Are you still enjoying your trip?"

"Yes! I can't wait to write about this place. There are so many activities to tell our readers about. From this barn dance to the cookie-decorating contest and the charity auction, and let's not forget Noel Navigators tomorrow. This town keeps Christmas hopping."

"Yes. It seems they do." Margie smiled. "My hometown is very much the same."

"Oh yeah? Where is that again?"

"Freedom Ridge."

"Right. I think you mentioned there is a ski resort there. I'm going to add that to my list to check out next Christmas."

Margie took one of her cards from her purse and handed it to her. "Call me if you decide to check it out. I'll put you in touch with my friend Jan. She has her finger on the pulse of everything in Freedom Ridge, so she can make sure you know exactly what is happening."

"Thanks." Leticia tucked the card into her handbag.

Chaz walked up and handed Margie a mug of steaming liquid then turned his attention to Leticia. "Sorry, I didn't see you here, or I would've grabbed one for you, too."

"I already had one. It was delicious."

Leticia's eyes sparkled with mischief as she looked from Margie to Chaz and back again. "I'll see you around, Margie. Don't get into too much trouble tonight."

~

THE BARN WAS HOPPING with music and dancing. He leaned close so Margie would be able to hear him. "Are you up for a two-step or is your knee still too sore?"

She grinned. "I thought you'd never get around to asking me to dance."

He held out his hand and when she placed hers inside his, he led her to the dance floor. "You're taller than most women I've danced with."

"Is that a bad thing?" she asked.

"It's not good or bad. It just is. It does make it easier to look into your eyes." He spun her away from him, and she executed the turn flawlessly. "You're not new to dancing, I see."

"John and I used to go country dancing at least once a month."

"And since he's been out of the picture?"

"I rarely get out of the house except for work."

"That makes me sad. You deserve better. Someone should be taking you out regularly."

"Thanks for saying that." Her eyes shone. "I am a grown woman though, so I could take myself out if I wanted."

He smiled. "Of course, you could, but clearly you don't."

When the band played the first strands of "Rockin' Years," he pulled Margie close, and they waltzed to the beat of the music. The words of the song left him longing for someone special to sit in the rocking chair beside his for the rest of his years. He wondered if Margie could be that someone.

After several dances, they made their way back to the table where she'd left her purse. Before she could sit, her cell vibrated. She fished it from her bag. "That's odd. I missed five calls." She scrolled through them, and the phone buzzed again in her hand. "I better take this. It must be important for them to keep calling." She walked away from the table with the phone pressed to her ear.

He wondered what could be so important that she would take the call while out on a first date. Then he chided himself. Back when he'd been working as a CEO, he'd have done the same thing. Life out here on the ranch had softened him to the harsh realities of the working world. Most people expected you to be available whenever they wanted to reach you. It didn't matter to them if it was a weekend or a holiday.

After a few minutes, Margie returned. Her face was flushed, and her eyes were clouded over and missing their usual spark.

"Is everything okay?"

"One of the houses I have listed was vandalized. It's a high-end home and the owners are livid. They think the pictures we posted of the house staged made it too obvious that it was empty, and nobody was living there."

"Did you call Freedom PD?"

"They've already been there. John's old partner pulled the case. I'm going to have to go home and do damage control."

A wave of disappointment rolled over him. He hated the idea of her leaving, but understood that she had a job to do.

"When will you leave?"

"First thing in the morning."

CHAPTER 9

MONDAY MORNING, MARGIE LEANED back in her chair and rubbed her forehead as she listened to Mrs. Hollingsworth voice her displeasure in no uncertain terms. Relief flooded through her when the call waiting beeped in. "I'm going to have to take this call that is coming through." She glanced at the screen and saw it was Mike Larson. "It's the detective handling the case, so I need to speak with him."

She clicked over. "Margie Crawford speaking."

"Marge, it's Mike."

"Hi, Mike. Please tell me you caught the vandals."

"No such luck."

"The homeowner is distraught, and she's blaming me."

"Sorry, but I think I'm about to make your day even worse."

"How is that possible?"

"I'm going to need a list of everyone you or any other real estate agents have shown the property to since it's been on the market."

"Everyone who has been through the property showed up with a preapproval letter or proof of funds. These weren't lookie-loos, they were serious potential buyers."

"We have to check them out."

"I'm not comfortable divulging that information."

"I understand where you're coming from, but we need to rule those people out. I'd like to do so as quietly as possible, but if you won't provide me with what I need, I will get it elsewhere, even if it means a warrant."

"Fine. I'll send you a list, but I'm doing so under protest."

As she compiled the list, her tension headache worsened. Mike was going down the wrong path looking for the vandals. If he kept digging in the wrong place, he'd never find out what really happened.

∾

A JINGLE ANNOUNCED HIS entrance as Chaz greeted Charlie. "Haven't seen you around in a while." He raised one of his bushy gray eyebrows questioningly.

"Barry likes to send the young guys to run most of the ranch's errands."

"I've noticed." Charlie tapped his knuckles on the counter. "So, what are you doing here now?"

"I need some bay lights to replace the old fluorescents in the barn and want to make sure I get the right thing. Didn't trust anyone else to get the right thing."

"LED?"

"That's the plan."

"Aisle seven."

He headed to the section Charlie indicated, found what he needed, and pulled four boxes off the shelf.

On his way back to the counter, he noticed a display of security cameras. Barry mentioned plans to have security install one by the tack room, but as far as Chaz knew it hadn't been done yet. He was going to have the extension ladder out to install the new lights, so he might as well get the cameras now, too. That way he could install them all today while he had it out.

He picked out what he needed and headed to the counter to check out.

"Barry's ready to increase security, huh?"

"He's got quite a bit of security looking out for the guest areas already, but there are no cameras watching the inventory."

"More cameras should be a good thing. Ready to check out?"

Chaz nodded and paid for his items. As he was driving out of town, he caught sight of a teenager leaving Bethany's Book Barn. The kid had a backpack slung over one shoulder. It looked like the same kid from the barn, but he couldn't be positive. He could go inside the bookshop and ask if anyone knew who it was, but no. He'd wait and see if anything else went missing, then he could check the cameras and see what turned up. Then if the teenager was on there, he'd get security to handle the matter.

MARGIE NEEDED TO MEET the plumber and the carpenter at the Hollingsworth property. The homeowners were still out of town, and they weren't comfortable with contractors they didn't know personally being in the house without supervision, so Margie would show up and make sure everything was locked up properly when they were finished with the work. It promised to be a boring day of sitting around and waiting for work to be finished. If it were her own house, she'd be far less inclined to stick around while they worked. Nobody liked having someone looking over their shoulder while they did their job.

Jan's smile greeted her when she pushed open the door to Stories and Scones. "You're back! I thought you were staying until after Christmas?"

Margie filled her friend in on the details of her return to town.

"Are you going back to Redemption Ranch?" Margie fixed her a pumpkin latte and grabbed her a pumpkin muffin topped with a dollop of cream cheese frosting.

She threw a twenty on the counter. "I'm not sure. Things out there were getting complicated. I might just cancel the remainder of my trip."

"Why would you do that? I thought you wanted the experience." Jan handed her back her change.

"Maybe. The horseback riding was fun, albeit challenging."

"So, what's the problem?"

"You have a minute to chat?"

Jan called into the back room, and a young woman took over at the counter while the two of them moved to a table.

"What's really going on?"

While she gathered her thoughts, Margie sipped her coffee, then pulled off a piece of muffin and popped it into her mouth. It was a perfect blend of sweet and spice. Yum. "I'm falling for Chaz. I know it's a terrible idea, so I don't think I should return. If things go wrong between us ... we have to think about the kids. It wouldn't be fair for us to make everything awkward for everyone."

"Whoa. Slow down, woman. Don't you think you and Chaz deserve a chance at happiness? Why would you assume things would go wrong?"

"In my experience, they always do."

"John is one man. A flawed man. All men are, but you can't compare him to Chaz. Those two guys are polar opposites."

"They both had positions where they felt they were invincible."

"One took a job as a cop because it gave him power over others. The other worked his way from opening a single storefront here in Freedom to owning a huge conglomerate of businesses. They are not the same thing."

"Money means power." She frowned. "I don't want a man to have that kind of influence over my life again."

"In a godly marriage, you shouldn't have to worry about the decisions your husband will make. If he's led by the Lord, he'll always have your best interest at heart."

"Fair point." She sighed. "Maybe that's the problem. I'm not spending enough time focused on the Lord to discern what He does or doesn't want me to do."

"Pray about it. If you're meant to go back and finish

this adventure, then do it. Fear doesn't come from God, so don't let it get in the way of finding out if there is something stronger than physical attraction between you and Chaz."

"I know you're right." She glanced at her cell phone screen. "I'd better get to the Hollingsworth house before the contractors show up."

Jan stood and Margie gave her a brief hug. "Thanks for taking the time to talk."

~

CHAZ STROLLED TOWARD HOME after installing the lights and cameras in the barn. The task had taken more out of him than he wished to admit. He wasn't getting any younger. He should probably consider cutting down to three days a week. Someone moved in the distance, and he recognized Paul coming fast on horseback. He hurried to the fence line to see what the other man needed.

"What's up?"

"Fence is down in the southern range. You think you can give me a hand with it? Already sent most of my men off to help with the Noel Navigator event."

"Sure thing. I'll take my truck and meet you out there. Are we going to need the fence puller?"

"Don't know. Got a call from a passerby that it was down, but not much in the way of details."

"I'll throw it in the truck and be there in a jiffy."

Paul nodded and headed off, and Chaz scratched the back of his neck. Whenever he considered working less, it seemed that more work fell into his lap whether he wanted it or not. It was the nature of the beast: The more you worked hard, the more you were relied upon and expected to work even harder. He chuckled to himself. His brother insisted on paying him for his work, but he donated his paychecks to Send the Light Missions. He already had more money than he could spend in his lifetime, and he wasn't sure why he worked at all. They pretended to need him at Redemption Ranch, but they'd gotten along fine before he'd moved back here, and they'd be fine long after he quit.

If he wanted to, he could return to Freedom and make a life with Margie. It was a crazy thought. They'd been on one date, and it hadn't ended well. But he could picture them married and visiting the grandchildren they would have, family dinners, and Christmas Eve services. He'd lost Suzanne so early in their marriage that he wasn't sure he knew how to be a husband to someone, but he might want to try if Margie was on the same page.

When he reached his house, he hopped into his truck and headed back to the barn to get the tools they needed. As he was entering, he saw someone sneak out of the back. It wasn't the best time to check the security cameras, but he'd make sure to take a look first thing in the morning.

Paul was looping his horse's reins around a fence post when he reached him.

Chaz frowned. "This is far worse than I expected. We're going to have to run temporary fence until we can get this fixed properly."

"This was deliberate."

The ground was rutted up like someone had been using

it for a demolition derby. "Why on earth would someone do this?" Chaz leaned against one of the few remaining fence posts.

"Joy riding?"

"I don't know. These posts are set in concrete. Getting them out took effort. Probably required a heavy-duty truck or tractor to drag them out of the ground. This was intentional, and there are so many places around here to go four-wheeling that this destruction feels more like vengeance than goofing off."

"Redemption Ranch does so much for the town, I can't imagine anyone hating us that much."

"Neither can I, but if someone does, we need to find out why."

Chapter 10

The following Sunday, Chaz tucked into one of the pews near the back as the pastor made his way to the podium. He tensed when he noticed Margie sitting across the aisle one row up. She hadn't mentioned returning to Redemption Ranch, so he'd assumed she planned on staying in Freedom. The piano started up and soon the choir was leading them in a congregational hymn. He'd have to wait an hour or more for the chance to talk with Margie. This time was reserved for God, and he needed to focus his attention where it belonged. He flipped through the pages until he found the proper hymn number and joined in as they sang "I Heard the Bells on Christmas Day."

As he closed his hymnal he thought about the words. He needed the reminder that God was alive and awake. All Chaz needed to do was trust Him with his future. If his son could follow God to a distant country, the least he could do was follow God across the state if that was what He required of him. And if, instead, it was God's will for him to remain single until his dying day, then he'd do that. If anything, it'd be easier. He was used to being alone.

The sermon echoed the first hymn as the pastor expounded on the message of the bells and what it would mean one day when Jesus returned and peace on Earth became more than a Christmastime slogan. It was a cohesive message that resonated deep within his being.

When the service ended and the worshipers scattered, he noticed Margie standing alone by the altar. He gave her a few moments to see if she intended to leave her burdens there. Time seemed to stand still as they stood in their respective places until she turned and locked eyes with him.

By the time she made it back down the aisle to where he stood, she was clutching her purse so tightly her knuckles turned white.

"Something the matter?" he asked.

"Convicting sermon."

He nodded. "We get a lot of them around here." He gestured for her to go ahead of him down the aisle. "I'm having brunch at Flapjacks with Barry and Connie. Care to join me?"

She bit her bottom lip. "Sure. That sounds nice."

He raised a brow. "Something's eating at you. Want to talk about it?"

"Not yet. No." She sighed. "I will when I'm ready."

"Is this you blowing me off and telling me you just want to be friends?"

She let out a forced laugh. "No. That isn't it."

"I'll pull my truck around and pick you up."

"I can walk with you."

"It's snowing, you'll get wet."

"You seem to forget I'm a native Coloradan. I'm used to the snow."

"And you forget that I'm a gentleman, and a gentleman gets the vehicle for a lady in inclement weather conditions."

She rolled her eyes. "All right then. I'll wait here."

~

MARGIE FILLED THE PLATE Chaz handed her with eggs, bacon, and french toast as they moved down the buffet line behind Barry and Connie. Her stomach clenched and she wasn't sure she'd be able to eat the food she'd taken.

Once they were settled into a booth, Chaz asked the Lord's blessing on their meals and everyone else dug in as she twirled her coffee cup in her hand. Jan had made good points when they'd talked. It had been a good reminder to consult the Lord about her plans and make sure she was following His will, but by the end of the day, she'd all but abandoned the idea. Giving up control was painful for her. If she put her life in God's hands, He might decide to turn it upside down like He'd done with Gage and Casey. She knew they were happy and were doing wonderful work leading people to Christ while also helping meet the villagers' physical needs, but she didn't want that kind of life.

This was the time in her life when things were supposed to slow down. She should be able to take it easy now that she had established a client base, and a reputation that carried weight with new customers. What would happen if God decided that she should move to Redemption and make a life with Chaz? Then what? Would she have to start over? Or would he want her to stay home and cook and clean? She knew she was getting ahead of herself with all her questions and what ifs, but neither of them was getting any younger, so if they were going to try the dating thing, neither of them would want to keep it casual long. Who was she kidding? It didn't even start out casually.

"Margie, you haven't touched your food. Is everything okay?" Connie asked.

She tried to laugh off the question. "Just lost in thought." She ate a forkful of cold eggs and grimaced. "I saw a flyer in the foyer at church for an art festival next weekend."

"Oh. That sounds like fun. I haven't heard of that yet. Is it Christmas themed?" Connie asked.

"I don't think so. Didn't look like it."

"What do you think, Barry? Want to go?"

"If you want to, dear."

Margie chuckled at his lack of enthusiasm.

Connie leaned forward. "What about you, Chaz?"

"I've never attended an art festival in my life."

Connie smiled. "Then this'll be a good time to start. You can go with Margie and let her expand your horizons."

Margie felt heat crawl up her neck. She didn't want Connie pressuring Chaz into taking her there.

"You're right. It's a brilliant opportunity to learn something about art appreciation." Chaz leaned toward Margie. "What time does it start?"

"Seven."

"I'll pick you up at half past six, then. Okay?"

She nodded but felt like crawling under the table. The only reason she'd brought up the topic was to change the subject to keep them from focusing on her lack of appetite.

Now she'd been mortified beyond repair after Chaz was basically told to ask her out again. Things between them were awkward enough without that added weirdness.

～

CHAZ STUCK A FROZEN dinner in the microwave and set the timer. It'd been a long day, and he didn't feel like making small talk through Sunday dinner with his brother's family. He was emotionally spent from worship service and brunch with Margie. She was acting strangely, and there was no telling what was behind her withdrawn mood. She'd been pensive rather than talkative, which was totally out of character for her. Then there was the moment when he'd seen her by the altar. Had he interrupted the time she needed to have with the Lord? He hoped not. The last thing he wanted to do was come between her and God.

After scarfing down his dinner, he flipped through the channels on the television until he found the Avalanche game and settled in to watch it.

As they were facing off to start the third period, his phone rang. His son.

"Gage. I wasn't expecting to hear from you. Is everything okay?"

"We're fine, but we had to leave the village with a dozen other believers last night. Islamic militants are conducting raids. A neighboring village was wiped out, but another village offered us safe haven."

"How do you know they won't raid that village next?"

"We don't."

"Son, maybe it's time to bring your wife home. Have you prayed about this?"

"I have. So has Casey, and we both believe God still wants us here. It's challenging, but we're okay. Don't mention any of this to Casey's mom. She'll be beside herself with worry if she hears what's happening."

Chaz could barely breathe as the stress of what was taking place on the other side of the world pressed down on him. His only son and his family were in mortal danger and there was absolutely nothing he could do to assist them. Not true. He could pray. And he would pray. "I won't mention anything to Margie."

"Thanks, Dad. I need to go. Casey wants to use the satellite phone to call her mom. I don't know when I'll be able to call again, so if I don't talk to you before then, Merry Christmas."

"Merry Christmas, son." Tears streamed down his cheeks as the call went silent. All the problems of the ranch and his relationships melted away. Gage and Casey were putting their life on the line for the Lord, and here he was struggling with whether he should be willing to uproot his life again even though he'd be moving to the same state in a familiar town where he knew everyone, and they all knew him. It was humbling.

～

ON WEDNESDAY AFTERNOON, MARGIE headed down to

the common area and chose a Christmas ball to decorate. She'd seen the event listed on the lodge's calendar of activities and figured it was something to do to get her mind off Casey's phone call. Her daughter hadn't come out and said what was bothering her, but her intuition was screaming that something was dreadfully wrong. She'd hit her knees the past three nights praying for God's mercy on Casey, Gage, and their unborn child. Now her injured knee was screaming its protests.

She spotted Leticia at one of the tables, so she took a seat by her and picked out some glittery bling to adorn the round ornament. A little sparkle might cheer her up some.

Leticia smiled in greeting. "I talked to my editor, and she's on board with me doing a piece on Freedom Ridge next Christmas."

"That's fabulous news! I'm so glad to hear it."

"I'm looking forward to this Christmas parade I read about on the town's website."

"That's nothing compared to the New Year's Eve ball, so make sure you stay long enough for that."

"I'll do that. Thanks for the tip." Leticia lowered her voice and leaned across the table. "I've noticed you've been a little down in the dumps since you returned to the lodge. Is everything all right?"

"Things at home were a mess. Someone broke into one of the houses I have listed, but the issue is mostly resolved now that the repairs have been made. We're still waiting on the police to catch the culprits, but I won't hold my breath." Talking about real estate was safe. Talking about her daughter and her feelings for Chaz was too personal.

"Anyone special at home to miss you this Christmas?" As the words came out of her mouth, she saw the hypocrisy. She expected others to open up, but she wanted to keep her side of the conversation at surface level.

"No. The last man I dated couldn't stand my work schedule, so he ended things before Christmas last year. I haven't bothered dating again."

"Why not?"

"I guess I'm not over him."

"I'm sorry."

"Don't be. I'm the one who chose my career. Now I have to live with my choice. Most of the time I'm happy enough."

Margie could relate to that. Most of the time she was content, but every once in a while, the loneliness would edge out that contentment, and she'd recognize her need for companionship.

CHAPTER 11

CHAZ PARKED AND ENTERED the lodge. Nearly a week had passed since the dreaded phone call from Gage, and he hadn't heard from him since. A lump formed in his throat, and he sent up a silent prayer.

He scanned the inside of the lodge and saw Margie seated by the fireplace with the same young woman she'd been chatting with at the barn dance. When he reached them, he grinned. She was dressed in tailored gray slacks paired with an ivory sweater and boots. Her hair was pulled back, and her makeup was flawless as usual. It was sophisticated but not pretentious. "You look stunning."

"Thank you." The woman standing with Margie was dressed in leggings and a long University of Tennessee sweatshirt. She patted her hair. "Kind of you to say." Then laughing, she pointed at Margie. "Oh. Were you talking to her?" She winked at them before walking away.

"Leticia is something else," Margie said.

At least now he had a name. "Sure is."

"You ready?"

"Whenever you are."

Together they walked out to the truck, and he opened

her door for her.

She frowned as she hauled herself in using the grab bar. "I get much older, and I won't be able to get into a truck this high."

Laughing, he jumped into the driver's side. "Nonsense. I have more than ten years on you, and I can get in here."

"You have some height on me, too. I'm sure that helps you climb inside."

"True, but maybe the height of my truck is a reason for you to appreciate your height since you are taller than most ladies."

"That's bologna, Chaz."

When they arrived at the community center downtown, Margie perused the artwork with the concentration of a true critic, while he stood back and admired her. She was a work of art in her own right. The years hadn't given her the worn-and-weary look he'd seen on so many faces. Something seemed to light her from within, and he hoped it might wear off on him.

❧

MARGIE SLOWLY MADE HER way around the community center, stopping at each piece and spending time with the ones that resonated with her. Regional artists had set up booths to display their work, and the room buzzed with excitement.

A painting of a Rocky Mountain landscape hung near the first display booth. Light played over snow-covered mountains, giving it an ethereal quality.

"I like that one." Chaz put his arm around her while she continued to stare.

"Me too." She smiled at him. She'd been worried that this date would be awkward, but it wasn't. They were comfortable together. Other than their children, they had little in common, but that didn't matter. He was here supporting her love of the arts even though he'd probably rather be watching a football game. She didn't even know if they had football on Saturdays, but she figured they must.

The next booth she stopped at was a sculpture of a young girl releasing a bird from her hand. Every feather was carved in intricate detail and the girl's expression was filled with radiant joy. "This sculpture is amazing. Reminds me to let go of all I've been holding tightly and trust God with all that I love."

"I can see that." He stood behind her, rubbing her shoulders.

She turned in his arms and lifted her face. "Thank you for bringing me here today. I could've come alone, but I'm glad you're with me."

"I'm happy to be here." His eyes twinkled, and she believed he meant the words.

They walked around some more before coming to a booth with pottery. She was drawn to a bud vase with a vine pattern etched into its surface. "This one is lovely."

Chaz smiled. "There is a lot of talent on display here today."

"Yes, there is." She grinned. "I see Connie over there. Shall we say hello?"

The feel of his hand on the small of her back left her longing to be more than a casual date to him. Were his feelings similar to hers, or was she crazy to think they could be more? They soon reached his sister-in-law, and Margie was engulfed in a warm hug.

Connie leaned over and whispered in her ear. "I'm glad you didn't back out of this date. You two are perfect for each other."

She let out a choked laugh. "Only time will tell."

CHAZ WALKED MARGIE TO the door but hesitated instead of going inside. Margie was opening it when he stopped her with a gentle hand on her arm. "I'm not sure I'm ready for the night to end."

"What did you have in mind? We drove all the way back from town, and there isn't much going on here at the ranch this time of night."

"You up for a walk?"

"Sure, but I think I'd like to change into something more comfortable first."

They moved inside, and she went upstairs while he wandered around the shared areas. It was a quiet night in the lodge. Most people were probably out on the town or up in their rooms.

Margie returned dressed in a pair of jeans and fur-lined boots. Even in casual attire the woman looked classy. He helped her into her white down coat and she tugged on a pair of matching gloves. She wasn't wearing a scarf, so he hoped it was because she wore a turtleneck sweater and not because she didn't like scarves. Otherwise, the gift he bought her wouldn't be appreciated. He was almost certain he'd seen her in them in the past though.

She placed her hand in his outstretched one, and they headed out into the night. The evening sky was dark and clear, showcasing the brilliance of the stars overhead. He tugged her closer as they walked, and she looped her arm around his waist. Having her tucked into his side felt right.

White lights adorned the building and the rock wall that separated the lodge from the rest of the ranch. He was reluctant to speak and ruin the moment, but at the same time, he thought they should probably talk.

He leaned against the wall and turned to look at her. "I'm glad you returned to Redemption Ridge."

"Me too." She tilted her chin up to meet his gaze.

He drew her into the circle of his arms and kissed her forehead. "I'm enjoying getting to know you better."

The corners of her mouth turned up in a wry smile. "I didn't think you liked me much when I got here."

"Let's be honest for a minute. You and I are worlds apart in communication styles."

"Meaning I can get kind of chatty, and you can be super quiet?"

"Something like that."

"Does that mean you didn't like me?"

"I wasn't sure what to make of you, but I never disliked you."

"Good to know."

"Something has been bothering you all night. Care to share?" He took both her hands in his and rubbed his thumbs along her fingers.

"I got a call from Casey last week, and it's been eating at me ever since."

"What did she have to say?"

"I'm sure you got the same call."

He needed to tread lightly to avoid saying too much. "I did, but I'd like to hear it from your perspective."

~

MARGIE SWALLOWED HARD AND fought to control the tears stinging the backs of her eyes. "I'm worried."

"Go on," he said.

"Casey said they were staying in another village for a while. I could tell there was something she wasn't telling me, and I'm scared."

"I'm worried, too."

"I've been up late every night praying, and I'm trying to give my fears over to God, but it's so hard to let go," she said.

He nodded and tugged her up against his chest. She let the tears she'd been holding back fall freely, and he held her while she sobbed. After several minutes, she pulled back and looked up at him. "Mascara must be running down my face in ugly streaks."

Shaking his head, he smiled and rubbed his thumbs gently under her eyes. "Only ran a tiny bit. You still look great." She was certain he was lying but appreciated his kindness anyway.

"We can't do anything about what's happening in Bangladesh other than pray. I've been doing a lot of that. God's probably tired of hearing my voice," he said.

"He would never get tired of listening to prayers from one of His children."

Chaz chuckled. "And praise the Lord for that." He gestured toward the fire pits the lodge kept lit in the evenings. "Care to sit and have a cup of hot apple cider? I can sneak into the kitchen and get us some."

"That sounds amazing." She took a seat by the fire and curled her legs up under her. It was a habit she really needed to break. As she grew older her legs fell asleep faster and her knees groaned in protest of the contortionist positions she placed them in, but it was so hard for her to feel comfortable with her legs on the ground that she couldn't seem to keep them there.

The night had taken a strange turn with their conversation about Gage and Casey. The man who had once intimidated her had shown a warm, gentle side she hadn't known he possessed. When he'd held her, she'd felt safe. It was an unfamiliar sensation. John had never given her that sense of security that Chaz did.

He returned with the apple cider and handed her the warm mug. Sweet with a hint of spice. Opposite the man who'd brought it. He was mostly spice with a hint of sweetness.

Chaz cleared his throat as he took his seat. "I was wondering if you'd consider attending Christmas Eve service with me Tuesday night."

"I'd love to."

"You'd love to consider it?"

She laughed. "I'd love to attend service with you." Tilting her head, she asked, "Does that mean I won't see you again until then?"

"I'm sensing you might not mind seeing me sooner than that."

"Are you?" The corners of her mouth lifted in a smile. "I can't imagine why you'd sense that."

"What are you doing after service tomorrow, Ms. Crawford?"

"I'll have to check my calendar." She winked.

"If we can escape my brother and his wife, I'd like to take you to lunch at Ridgeline Grill."

"Just the two of us?"

He nodded.

"Sounds perfect."

CHAPTER 12

MARGIE SET HER KINDLE back down on the bedside table. She couldn't concentrate on the words. Her mind kept drifting back to Chaz. Was he as emotionally invested as she was? His request to take her out again hadn't been at anyone else's prompting this time, so he must like her, but a niggling doubt wouldn't let go. What if she fell in love with Chaz but later found out she wasn't enough for him?

Despite the passage of time and the healing she found in Christ, she couldn't completely dispel herself of the notion that she was unlovable. That it was somehow her fault John had strayed. No, it was far worse than straying, he'd forced himself on young girls. His crimes weren't her fault, and she knew that in her head. She'd tried to follow the example of a good wife set in Proverbs thirty-one though she knew she often fell short.

Her hope was in the Lord. If this new relationship with Chaz had any chance of becoming something beautiful, it would be because they both leaned on God in good times and bad.

How she could even be thinking of herself when her only child faced some unknown danger that she wouldn't even share with her, she didn't understand. Yet her heart found a way to multi-task and allow her to feel new and wonderful things while also hurting for Casey and Gage.

Lifting the Kindle again, she forced herself to focus on the words on the screen. She hadn't brought her leather Bible with her to Redemption, so she read the beautiful words of the King James Version on her device. While she missed the feel of the paper under her fingers as she read, she appreciated the lightweight device, and the best part was the ability to make the text bigger as her eyes grew tired. A problem that happened more and more as time went on.

She turned her eyes toward the ceiling and spoke to her Creator. "Is this your will, Lord? Are Chaz and I being given a second chance at love?" Only silence answered her, but in her heart, she felt the truth. God had brought her here for a reason.

∽

CHAZ SHUFFLED INTO CHURCH with less than two minutes to spare and tucked into the pew beside Margie. She smiled by way of greeting. He wasn't used to cutting it so close, but when he'd gone to check the camera in the tack room, he'd found the memory card had been removed, so he'd stopped by the security office to ask them to take care of the problem. It was time he stopped trying to micromanage everything. It wasn't even his ranch, and he was supposed to be retired. Now was as good a time as any to think about his future and decide if he was going to build on his own property outside of Redemption or if he should consider returning to Freedom Ridge.

While he didn't want to make the decision solely based on a new relationship that might not even work out, he also didn't want to throw away the chance of something special with Margie. He could ask her about properties in Freedom. Who better to talk to about real estate than the agent he'd worked with when he lived there? And bringing it up might give him a feel for how she'd feel about having him close.

Maybe it was all too much, too soon. He needed to talk to someone. To have a sounding board to run things by. Barry would work. They were going to be on the southern range to oversee the repair crew in the morning. Another example of something he didn't need to be doing. There was no reason at all that his brother couldn't handle that by himself, but he wanted Chaz to feel needed, so he kept giving him work to do. Jobs that could be done by someone else. It wasn't that he wanted to leave the ranch altogether, he enjoyed being there, but he needed a manageable schedule that would allow him to do more than work. And if he decided to move back to Freedom, he might need to find something to keep him busy there. He could go back to work at Freedom Mountaineering. Carly would *love* that. Shaking his head at the thought, he forced himself to focus on what the pastor was saying. Something about there being a time for all things under the sun. It was from Ecclesiastes. Yes. Maybe this was his time for love. Only God knew for sure.

MARGIE AND CHAZ FOLLOWED as the host showed them to a table. It was a terrific location in the back, away from the entrance and the kitchen doors. Chaz pulled out her chair and waited for her to sit, then sat across from her.

She perused her menu and settled on the broiled trout. "Let me guess, prime rib?"

"How'd ya know?"

"You seem like a steak kind of guy."

"What did you decide on?"

"I'm going to have the trout with zucchini and rice pilaf."

He made a face. "Yuck."

"Sounds delicious to me."

"So, I've been thinking..."

"That's a scary thought."

He frowned. "You're not making this easy."

"Sorry." She made a gesture of zipping her lips and sat silently with her hands folded on the table.

"What if I move back to Freedom? Do you think there are decent properties available there that I might be interested in?"

"Why on earth would you go back? You seem happy here."

He gave her a pointed look, and warmth flooded her face. "Oh. No. You wouldn't want to do that. It's too soon. We don't know if it'll work out."

"Margie, I'm sixty-seven years old and, as you know, I've already had the scare of a brain tumor. I don't have time to date for years before deciding if I'm interested in a woman. If there is something between us, I don't want you running back to your life and leaving me behind."

"But what if it doesn't work and you uproot your whole life?"

"Right now, it's just something I'm considering. I haven't committed to anything. Now back to my original question. Are there properties or not?"

"You might like the one I had to go back to town to deal with. It's a beautiful ski chalet in a great neighborhood."

"Perfect. I'd like to see it after Christmas."

"All right." She squeezed lemon into her water and took a long sip. "I'll arrange it."

∼

CHAZ DROVE TO THE southern range early to spend time in prayer before Barry arrived. He still hadn't heard from Gage since his phone call eight days earlier, and it was becoming more and more difficult to hold his fears at bay. If something happened to them, and he hadn't shared what he knew with Margie, she'd never forgive him. Yet he'd made a promise to his son, and he intended to keep it.

He'd only had a few minutes of quiet reflection with the Lord when Paul's truck came rumbling in. The other man joined him on the worksite. "You're early."

"Yeah," Chaz said.

"How's it going with you and that attractive guest of ours?"

"Margie?"

"That's the one."

"I hope it's going well. She joined me for lunch yesterday, and we're attending Christmas Eve service together tomorrow night."

Paul slapped him on the back. "That's disappointing. She'd rather have an old man like you than a young fellow like me, I guess."

"You're not that young, Paul."

"Not that old either. Probably much closer to her age than you are." He grinned. "Seriously though, I'm glad things are working out. She seems like a great gal. I'm happy for you."

"Thanks. I appreciate that." He sighed. He'd been planning to talk things over with Barry, but Paul might be a better choice for a sounding board. "I'm thinking about making a move to let her know I'm serious. Maybe not a ring quite yet, but something big enough to show her that I'm ready for that kind of a commitment."

"Why not go all out and get the ring? If she says yes, you can start your life together now. Why wait?"

He rubbed the tension from his neck as he thought about Paul's suggestion. "You might be right. Maybe I'll do that."

"If she says no, send her back my way."

"There is no chance of that happening in this lifetime, buddy."

CHAPTER 13

CHRISTMAS EVE MORNING, CHAZ stepped outside and let the cool morning air wash over him. It had been another restless night, but today was a day to celebrate the birth of Christ, and he intended to make the most of it. First thing on his schedule was a trip up the mountain to choose a tree. When the kids were growing up, they cut a fresh one on Christmas Eve morning and then brought it home and decorated it. He hadn't bothered since the kids left home, but he'd see if Margie would revive the tradition with him.

He drove to the lodge and found her inside having breakfast in the dining room, so he grabbed himself a coffee and pastry and joined her at the table she was sharing with Leticia and another woman. "Want to go for a ride?"

"My mama taught me better than to get in a car with strange men." Leticia rolled her eyes and laughed.

Margie grinned. "Where to? My mama taught me better than to accept an invitation without finding out the destination first."

"To cut down a Christmas tree."

"Aren't you a little late for that? It's Christmas Eve, in case you hadn't noticed."

"That's when I get my tree."

"Sure. I'd be glad to join you."

Twenty minutes later, they were headed up the mountain on a curvy, snow-dusted road. "Thanks for coming."

"Happy to."

"Haven't done this since the kids grew up."

"Why not?"

"It felt silly to bother."

~

MARGIE STUDIED THE MAN beside her. He hadn't shaved that morning, so he had a day's growth of stubble that gave off a rugged vibe and she found herself liking it more than she would've expected. She always claimed to like a clean-shaven man, but he had that mountain-man attraction down to a science.

In the past thirty minutes, he'd grown quiet and reflective as they wound their way through the mountain roads to what she assumed was a tree farm. The last time she'd been close to a tree farm was when she'd been held captive on the property that butted up against Evergreen Ranch on the outskirts of Freedom Ridge. A shudder rippled through her at the memory. She'd thought she would die in that hole in the ground: An animal trap, they told her when they pulled her out. Gage had been her rescuer, and she'd thought she couldn't be more grateful until she learned that the same man who'd abducted her had taken Casey. When Casey made it back to Freedom Ridge Resort safely,

Margie understood for the first time the depth of gratitude she could feel to another human being.

Chaz pulled onto a wooded property with a partially frozen lake and a decrepit house that looked like it might fall down any minute. Her eyes widened. It wasn't a tree farm. "Where are we?"

"This is my property. Belonged to my parents. My mother abandoned it when she remarried Barry's dad, but she left it to me when she died. I've been thinking about building a house on it, but if I come back to Freedom that won't happen."

"I love it."

"Me too." He smiled, but there was sadness in it. "I thought we could choose a tree from here. It'll hold more significance that way."

She hadn't known that Chaz had a sentimental side, but she found it endearing. "That's a terrific idea."

They wandered around looking for a nice tree that would fit inside the tiny adobe cottage Chaz had made his home since he'd moved to the ranch.

"This one might be perfect, what do you think?" she asked.

"I think it's lovely, but not as lovely as the woman who chose it."

"You're making me blush."

"And the color looks good on you."

W‌HEN THEY ARRIVED BACK at the ranch, Chaz realized he'd given all his old ornaments to Carly, so he hadn't brought any with him when he'd moved, so they stopped by the Reynolds' property to borrow a box of their decorations.

Connie gestured for them to come in and grinned at her brother-in-law. "I'm glad you called. I have several boxes of ornaments since I like to change up the colors on the fancy tree each year to keep it interesting."

"Fancy tree?" Margie cocked her head to the side.

Barry joined them. "That would be the tree that guests see when we're entertaining. It's in the living room, and it's decorated flawlessly, showcasing my wife's talent for design, but the tree that we all love best is in the den. It's covered in memories."

"Let me guess, ornaments handmade by your children over the years?" Margie asked.

"Yes, those plus some mementos from vacations and special moments in our lives."

"Sounds perfect."

Connie's eyes held an extra sparkle as she looked up at her husband and then back at them. "It is. What colors were you two thinking? Blue and white. Crimson and gold. Green and peach."

"They all sound wonderful. What do you think, Chaz?"

"You choose." He wanted everything to be perfect for her. So might as well let her pick.

"Let's go with the blue and white. Blue is Casey's favorite color."

Connie handed them a box of ornaments and they took

them back to the house and got to work decorating the tree.

∼

MARGIE STOOD BESIDE CHAZ as he lifted the silver star from the box. "Want to put this on top?"

"You're taller, you do it."

"The tree isn't that tall."

"You had to cut the bottom to fit it in here."

He placed the star on the top and it tilted sideways. She couldn't hold back a laugh. "You need to straighten it."

He folded one of the neighboring branches and tucked it inside the base of the star to get it to stand straighter. "Not bad."

"Still not straight," she said.

"Since you're the expert, you can fix it." He grabbed a step stool from beside his refrigerator and set it up for her.

She looked at it skeptically. "I'm going to break my neck if I do this."

"No, you're not. I'll catch you if you fall."

He held out his hand, and she climbed the few steps, then reached out to fix the star. "Better?"

"It needs to lean a little more to the left," he said.

She adjusted it, and as she was straightening, she lost her balance.

"I've got you." His hands steadied her by her waist, and the warmth of his hands seeped through her thin sweater.

"Thanks." She stepped down and stood beside him, admiring their work. "We did it."

"Yes, we did. Shall we plug the lights in?"

A knock on the door pulled them out of the moment. Chaz hurried to answer it.

❧

WHEN CHAZ OPENED THE door, his jaw dropped, and he tugged his son into a bone-crushing hug. "You're home."

Weariness etched Gage's features. "Sorry, I didn't have time to call. Send the Light Missions insisted we come home on furlough early."

Margie came into view and took a turn hugging Gage then looked past him. "I knew something was terribly wrong. They were worried for your safety, weren't they?"

He nodded but didn't elaborate.

"Is Casey with you?" she asked.

"She's at the lodge where she thought she'd find her mother, but I see you're hanging out with my dad." Gage laughed. "Looks like you two are getting along well."

"Come on. Let's go fetch Casey," Chaz said.

"You two stay here. I'll go get her in the rental. I left it running since I thought I'd be picking Dad up and bringing him back to the lodge."

"I'm going with you! I can't wait that long to see Casey." Margie pulled on her coat as she spoke.

"I'll get some hot chocolate ready for everyone." He focused on Gage. When you get back here, you and your wife can regale us with stories of your adventures abroad."

"Will do, Dad. We'll be right back."

Chaz nodded. When they were gone, he went into his tiny kitchen and set to work making the hot chocolate. When he was in town, he'd picked up instant cocoa packs, along with unsweetened cocoa, a pack of mini-marshmallows, and a can of whipped cream so he could make it for Margie the way he used to make it for his kids. But having Gage here made the moment even more perfect. Now he wished Carly was coming now instead of waiting until tomorrow.

They only had about two hours left before service started. He hoped Margie would still want to join him, but he would understand if she wanted to skip it. Although, he didn't see Gage and Casey missing service. They were faithful warriors for Christ, so he imagined they'd want to attend despite the exhaustion they must both be feeling.

～

CASEY TACKLED MARGIE AS she entered the lodge. "Where were you?!"

"With your father-in-law."

"Interesting development."

"How are you feeling? I can't believe you're going to be a mother."

"I know. I'm glad I get to be home for the pregnancy. I'll admit I was fearful. God provides our needs, I know that, but being so far away from proper medical care scared me. If something went wrong, I'd be relying on God alone."

"Sometimes that's the point," Gage said.

"But this time, He provided by bringing us home for a season. I won't complain."

"Neither will I, darling." Gage tugged Casey close and kissed her neck.

Margie locked eyes with Gage. "Let's head back over. Your dad is making us all some hot chocolate. We have a couple of hours before I need to be back here to get ready for Christmas Eve service."

"Why don't you get ready now, and then we'll just head over right from Dad's house?" Gage asked.

It would save time. "All right. I'll do that." She met her daughter's stare. "Want to come upstairs and help me pick out a nice outfit that'll be appropriate for my date with your father-in-law?"

Casey squealed. "It's supposed to be a date, and we're interrupting?"

"I don't think either one of us would be able to think of any interruption we would welcome more than having the two of you join us tonight. We've both been worried sick this past week."

"Did Dad tell you about the raids? We told him not to," Gage said.

"Raids? No. He didn't say a word." She clenched her jaw. If he'd known their children were in danger, he should've told her.

"Don't get mad at him. We asked him not to tell you since I knew you wouldn't be able to concentrate on anything else if you thought we were in more danger than usual." Casey took her hand and pulled her up the stairs behind her. "His silence was nothing more than keeping a confidence. It's an admirable quality to be able to stay silent when it's hard. You'll be able to trust him with things you don't want repeated, too."

Casey had a point. Margie scooted around her and opened the room door. "If we're going to be sitting around for a couple of hours first, I think maybe slacks would be best."

"Don't be a fuddy duddy, Mom. How about a long skirt. You'll still be comfortable, but you'll also look gorgeous." Casey shuffled around hangers until she found something and then laid it out on the bed. "How about this?"

She'd chosen a dark-green skirt that flared at the waist. Then she went to the dresser and pulled out a peach sweater. "These colors look good together."

Margie never would have placed the two items together, but she remembered Connie saying something about peach and green ornaments going together, so maybe it worked. She'd take Casey's word for it. She got down on her knees and pulled her Lucchese boots out from under the bed. "Will these work?"

Casey nodded. "You'll definitely turn his head in that outfit."

Margie sat on the edge of the bed. "Things might be moving a little too fast. He's talking about uprooting his life and moving back to Freedom."

"Don't you want that?"

"Honestly, I don't know. I like him a lot, but he's a different person here. I'm falling in love with Redemption Chaz. Not Freedom Ridge's Martin Charles Buchanan."

"He's the same man, Mom."

"I know. But he acts differently."

"Don't you think that's because the two of you are growing closer?"

"I'm sure that's part of it."

"Did you ever consider moving here?"

"We just started seeing each other. It would be crazy for me to uproot my whole life and leave a career I love for a man."

"Not if you love him." The words were spoken softly, but their impact slammed into her like a two-ton bomb.

CHAPTER 14

MARGIE KICKED OFF HER boots and tucked her feet up under her, making herself comfortable beside Chaz. She hadn't yet broached the subject of him holding back information from her, but she knew they would need to address it eventually. Tonight and tomorrow, there would be a reprieve though. It was time to celebrate Christ's coming to redeem man, and a time to celebrate the return of their children. Bringing conflict into the festive atmosphere would only serve to ruin what could be an amazing and memorable night.

"I'm looking forward to a traditional Christmas Eve service." Casey sat cross-legged on the floor with her cup of cocoa clasped in her hands.

Gage sat beside her. "Me too."

"You know, I do have furniture," Chaz said from his spot beside Margie.

"We're used to sitting on the ground. Our services are held in the open air, and we all sit on the ground in a circle. It's good, but it'll be nice to have a pew to sit on tonight."

Guilt gnawed at Margie's gut for hating the hardness of the uncomfortable pews with only a thin cushion to make them bearable. On the other side of the world, they didn't have such simple luxuries. "How are you feeling, hon? Any morning sickness."

"I think I'm finally past it. It was awful."

Margie grimaced. "I had it pretty bad with you, too."

"Suzanne didn't have it with either of our children."

She almost replied with a comment about what a blessing it would be to avoid morning sickness, but shortly after giving birth to her children, Suzanne had been called home to be with the Lord, so Margie chose to remain silent.

"Mom would've been glad to see that you put the tree up."

"You think so?"

"I do." Gage smiled. "You haven't had one since Carly's last year of high school, have you?"

He shook his head. "Didn't see the point once she went off to culinary school."

"It's nice to see you enjoying the holidays again, Dad."

∽

CHAZ WAITED FOR GAGE, Casey, and Margie to file into the pew then took the aisle seat beside Margie. He was surprised when she reached for his hand. The room was too dark for reading, so neither of them opened the pew Bibles when the scripture was read aloud. When the pastor took his seat, the choir opened their portion of the service with a medley of traditional Christmas hymns. They harmonized beautifully, and he found himself closing his eyes to experience the music more fully. Margie rested her head against his shoulder, and he imagined she was enjoying the service as much as he was. When he glanced over, he saw tears streaming down her face, and he eyed her questioningly. She turned to him with a wobbly smile.

"I'm just grateful they're here and safe." She looked at Gage and Casey.

Tears burned the back of his own eyes. He felt the same way. God had answered their prayers and brought them peace. Now they would enjoy the blessing of seeing their grandchild as soon as he or she was born. It was an amazing gift, and he was grateful to God for bringing it about. But his heart still ached for the Christians suffering persecution that remained in Bangladesh and so many other countries where they couldn't worship freely. It was a stark contrast to the freedoms they took for granted. He lifted Margie's hand to his lips and kissed her palm. The move seemed to surprise her, but she scooted closer, so he took it to mean she hadn't minded at all.

As the service drew to an end, the congregation joined the choir and sang "Silent Night." The walk to the car was spent in quiet contemplation, each of them lost in their own thoughts. At least that's how it appeared to Chaz.

They piled into the rental car and Gage drove them back to the ranch. "Want to come over and watch a Christmas movie?"

"We're beat." Gage pulled up to drop Chaz off and looked to Casey to see if she agreed. "I think we're going to retire to our room at the lodge. We'll see you in the morning."

"I'll join you for that movie." Margie's voice had a smile in it. "But if I do, we have to watch 'White Christmas.'"

"You have yourself a deal, woman."

She gave Gage and Casey kisses on their cheeks and climbed out of the car.

∾

MARGIE SAT BESIDE CHAZ, a bowl of popcorn between them. She couldn't believe he'd really put "White Christmas" on. She loved the old movie but didn't think it would be one of his favorites. It was one of the many ways she'd already seen him compromise. Even knowing he was nothing like John, she found herself constantly wondering when he would do something to hurt her. But he hadn't. Even when he'd withheld information, it hadn't been done spitefully, and he'd never lied to her. Not as far as she could tell. Well, except when he told her she looked good with mascara running down her face. That had to be a lie, no doubt.

He lifted the bowl from between them and set it on the coffee table. "Come closer."

Butterflies danced in her stomach at the prospect of sitting close to him. They'd sat close together in church, but they hadn't been alone.

"I promise to behave."

She felt her face flaming at his words, but she scooted closer to him on the couch, and he draped his arm around her. But true to his word, that was all he did. When the movie was over, he stood and stretched. "I have a gift for you. I was going to wait until tomorrow, but we'll be sharing Christmas with the kids, and I want to give this to you when we're alone."

Her stomach knotted in anticipation, wondering what on earth he could possibly have gotten her that he wanted to give it to her in private. At least it wasn't a ring. The box he handed her was large and tall.

"I didn't bring your gift over with me."

"I don't need a gift, and I have another small gift to give you tomorrow when we're with the kids. This one is more personal."

She carefully removed the paper, trying not to destroy it, but he made it difficult with the abundance of tape he'd used. When she unfolded the flap and peered inside, she felt tears stinging her eyes once more. It was an emotional day, and he made sure to keep it that way. "You bought it for me."

"The way you described it, I had to. The piece belongs with you."

She traced the feathers on the bird in the little girl's hand, then set the sculpture down on the table. "Thank you. You don't know how much this gift means to me."

He tilted her chin up, so she was forced to look into his eyes. "I think I do."

The moment was fraught with tension, and she couldn't take it much longer. She wove her arms around his neck. "Are you going to kiss me or not?"

His lips descended on hers, and she felt every bit of pent-up tension in their shared kiss. There was no more doubt in her mind that he felt the same way about her that she did about him. His kiss told her all she needed to know.

～

CHAZ WAS HEADED BACK to his truck after walking Margie to the door of the lodge when he noticed someone crawling around in the shadows near the fire pits. "Hey. Everything okay over there?" He walked over to check it out. It was the same young man he'd seen in the barn on two occasions. The kid he'd seen leaving Bethany's Book Barn the day he'd gone to the hardware store. The boy didn't look good. Blood was caked on his face and covered his clothing. One eye was swollen shut, and he had a fat lip. He'd been badly beaten. If he were to guess, he'd say he'd been jumped by more than one person or beaten with brass knuckles. The young man needed help fast. He knelt beside the boy. He was trying to pull himself up. He'd figured the kid was involved in some kind of petty larceny but couldn't imagine that had led to this savage beating. But answers would have to wait. "Come on. We need to get you to the hospital." He helped the kid up and got him into the truck then sped to Mercy Regional Hospital instead of calling an ambulance. He was pretty sure he could get there faster.

When they pulled up outside the emergency room, he tried to get the kid to wake up enough to talk. "Can you tell me your name? They're going to ask me who you are when we get inside."

"I don't need a hospital. Just take me home."

"No way. If my son were in this kind of condition, I'd

expect the person who found him that way to get him help. That's what we're going to do, but it would help if you'd tell me your name and where you live."

"Kyle Shepherd. I live in the apartment above my mom's store."

"Who is your mom?"

"Bethany Shepherd. She owns Bethany's Book Barn."

That explained his seeing him there.

"I won't ask how you wound up at the lodge tonight." Chaz shook his head. "We'll talk more when you're better. In the meantime, let's get you some help."

CHAPTER 15

CHAZ SANK INTO A chair in the waiting room of Mercy Regional Hospital's emergency department and dialed the number he'd finally gotten for Bethany Shepherd. She was unlisted and had no personal social media accounts that he could find. When he gave up trying to find it on his own, he called Margie. She agreed to call her friend, the famous author, to see if he had it. And thankfully, he did.

"Mrs. Shepherd."

There was shuffling on the other end of the line. "It's Miss."

"Miss. My apologies. I'm Martin Charles Buchanan. I work at Redemption Ranch."

"Do you always call people this late, Mr. Buchanan?"

"No, ma'am."

"How did you even get this number?"

"With much difficulty I assure you. If you'll let me explain why I'm calling?"

"I'm listening."

"I'm here at Mercy Regional Hospital with your son."

"Kyle is in the hospital!? Is he all right?"

"I think maybe you should come down here. They want

you to sign some papers, agreeing to allow treatment."

"Put Kyle on the line."

"I'm afraid I can't do that. He was barely conscious when I brought him here, and now he's in the back with the doctors. He's out of it."

"What happened to him?"

"I'm not entirely sure. I found him near Redemption Lodge and brought him here, but he was savagely beaten."

"I'll be right there."

After disconnecting the call, he leaned his head back and closed his eyes. Looked like he was in for another night of intense prayer. He thanked the Lord for counting him worthy to intercede on the boy's behalf.

~

MARGIE POUNDED HER PILLOW into submission and rested her head on it once more. Sleep eluded her. The phone call from Chaz about Bethany Shepherd's son had rattled her. Why on earth would someone harm the boy? She didn't know the woman, but her heart went out to her all the same. Having something terrible happen to your child tore a parent apart. The Lord had seen fit to give her a short reprieve from the stress of having Casey in Bangladesh, and she was grateful for that.

Bethany had her son with her here in Redemption, yet someone had seen fit to leave him lying on the ground beaten and discarded like he wasn't even a human being. The thought disgusted her. Who would do something so vile to another person? For what purpose?

Memories rolled over her of Christmas when Casey was a young girl and the love and laughter that filled their home. Unbidden, the darker memories came of their first Christmas without John and the confusion in Casey's eyes as she tried to understand how the man she'd believed was a hero had torn apart her world with his selfish actions. Margie forced herself to pray for the Shepherds and get the painful memories out of her head. She'd chosen to forgive John for the pain he'd caused her and Casey, and to let the past stay in the past. It didn't do any good to dwell on things that couldn't be changed.

She rolled over and faced the clock. It was Christmas day. The sun hadn't risen yet, but it would soon, and she needed to get some sleep before it did. Closing her eyes, she prayed for Bethany, Kyle, Casey, and for herself.

～

CHAZ ARRIVED HOME AS the sun rose over the red rock mountains. A beautiful sight to be sure, but he needed sleep if he was to make it through the holiday festivities. A few hours would suffice, but he had to get some rest. He brushed his teeth and then fell onto the bed without bothering to change his clothes.

Four hours later a knock on his door woke him, and he went to answer it.

"You look terrible." Gage pushed past him.

He smiled. "Thanks, son. Appreciate it."

"Why are you still in yesterday's clothes?"

"Spent the night in the hospital."

"What!? And you didn't have someone get me? Are you okay? Is it another tumor?"

"I'm fine. It wasn't me I was there for. Have a seat while I make some coffee."

He set the pot to brewing then took a seat at the table. "When I dropped Margie off at the lodge last night there was a teenager outside that had been brutally beaten. I took him to the hospital and stayed until the doctors were able to tell us he was going to make it."

"That's awful."

Chaz nodded. "But about today, what are your plans? Dinner here?"

"That's what I came over to talk about. Uncle Barry and Aunt Connie want us all to come to the house for Christmas dinner. Aunt Connie said you told her you were going to have a quiet dinner at the house, but she thought I might be able to convince you to go to their house."

"Fine, as long as your sister and her husband are invited."

"They are."

"And Margie."

"I'm sure that can be arranged."

"Very well. It's dinner at the Reynolds' house. Probably for the best since this place is entirely too small to entertain all those people."

Gage grinned. "I've been entertaining in a bamboo hut, so this feels like a mansion."

"I don't know how you do it." Chaz sighed. "I'd be lost without my modern conveniences."

"Most of the time, I enjoy the tranquility of our life there, but it hasn't been so tranquil these past few weeks."

"I guess not. Want to talk about it?"

"Maybe later. Today is about thanking God for sending His son, and I want to keep the focus where it belongs."

Chaz clasped his son's shoulder and then got up to pour the coffee.

∽

CHAZ ENTERED THE LODGE, but instead of seeking out Margie, he headed down the hall to his left that led to the security office. He used his badge to let himself in and focused on the red-haired man monitoring the dozens of screens lining the walls. "Hey, Milo."

"Need something, Mr. Buchanan?"

"There was an incident. I need you to see if you can find any footage of it."

"Do you know the time and location by any chance?"

"Likely near the lodge sometime between five and eleven last night."

Milo furrowed his brow. "That's a large window of time."

"I know. Start at eleven and work your way backward."

"Mind me asking what I'm looking for?"

"A teenager took a beating. One that landed him in the hospital, fighting for his life."

The man's hazel eyes clouded over. "Oh. I don't know how we missed something like that."

"I'm not even sure it took place on the property, but I found him by the lodge."

"I'll get right on it."

"I won't stand over your shoulder while you work. I'll check back later if I don't hear from you first."

Milo nodded in silent appreciation.

"There is one other thing I should probably mention." Chaz scratched his chin.

"What's that?"

"I think the kid who took the beating has been stealing from the ranch. According to my inventory sheets, it's enough to be a felony, but I don't think Barry or Cassie will want to press charges provided the kid is willing to work off his debt once he's healed up." He handed him a list with the dates and times he'd seen the young man in the past. "You might want to see if anyone else was hanging around on these dates and times, too. I'm not sure what this kid got himself into, but we should do what we can to help the cops get the people who did this to him."

"You're probably right about the bosses. They're the forgiving sort."

Chaz nodded. "I'll let you get to work. Call if you find something."

❧

MARGIE DRESSED IN A pair of ivory slacks and a burgundy sweater. For a touch of whimsy, she added a pair of snowman earrings to her ensemble. Connie said they were eating around five. Gage and Casey had wanted to participate in all the activities the lodge had planned to make sure the guests enjoyed the holiday, so she'd been going non-stop since she got out of bed. And she was doing it purely on caffeine and prayer, because she'd had precious little sleep the night before.

A knock on her door startled her. Gage and Casey said they'd meet her downstairs at quarter of five. She opened the door to find Chaz. The lines around his eyes seemed deeper than yesterday, making it clear he hadn't had much rest either.

"Hi," he said.

"Hey."

"Are you going to invite me in?"

She laughed as she realized she had been standing there staring at him. "Sure. Come on in."

"I know we're supposed to meet at my brother's house, but I was hoping to have a few minutes of time alone with you today, and once we get there, there will be no getting out until close to midnight."

"I hope you're wrong. I'm exhausted." A yawn punctuated her sentence.

"Me too." He followed her to the seating area and sat down. "You're going home after Christmas, aren't you?"

"That was the plan, but I thought I might extend my stay until New Year's. After all, I had to go home for a few days to deal with that real estate emergency."

He grinned. "I'm glad you're staying for a while. When you get back though, I do want to see that property you mentioned."

Margie nodded and bit her bottom lip. "Okay." She wanted to tell him that she would find a job here, so he wouldn't have to leave this place he loved behind, but she couldn't bring herself to make the commitment when they'd only been on a few dates. What if he changed his mind after she'd already relocated?

CHAPTER 16

GAGE AND CASEY ARRIVED at the Reynolds' residence at the same time as Chaz and Margie. Rather than knocking, Chaz pushed open the door at his brother's house and held it while they entered. The house was abuzz with activity, so it took a moment for Connie to notice they'd arrived.

"Come on into the living room and get settled. Dinner will be served in about fifteen minutes."

"Zeke," Chaz looked at his nephew. "Have you met Margie?"

"Haven't had the pleasure." Zeke smiled. "Nice to meet you."

"I'm sure you remember my nephew, Gideon, from your hike." Chaz winked at her.

"I'll probably never forget that tumble down the hill." Margie laughed. "It was a nice hike until that moment, anyway."

"Glad you weren't permanently damaged."

"Don't let my brothers turn on the charm, Margie," Cassie said.

Those cousins of mine are nothing but trouble," Carly said.

"Look who's talking." Gideon mussed Carly's hair.

"Hey!" Carly finger combed her hair back into place. "You see what I'm talking about? Pure trouble. Nothing but."

"Gideon's right. Carly was more difficult than the rest of us combined," Cassie said.

"I have to agree." Gage smiled down at his sister.

"I'm feeling outnumbered."

After a few more minutes of conversation and teasing banter, Connie came in. "Why don't we all take our seats at the table?"

They all filed in and sat around the enormous dining table.

"I see you put the leaves into the table," Zeke said.

"Wanted to enjoy a sit-down meal rather than go buffet style," Connie said.

"Everything looks delicious," Margie said.

Chaz chuckled. "That's because it is."

Connie's eyes twinkled. "And calories don't count on Christmas." She turned to her husband. "You want to say grace, dear?"

Barry asked the blessing, and then they passed the bowls around family style.

"You look tired, Dad," Gage said.

"I could say the same about you, son."

"Yes, but you don't have jet lag from flying halfway around the world."

"That's true. Just had a rough night last night."

"I heard about the Shepherd boy. Is he going to be okay?" Barry asked.

"He was stable by the time I left the hospital."

"That's good news."

Chaz nodded. "What are everyone's plans for New Year's?"

"We're talking about going to the charity concert at the Mesa. I heard Mia Rose is performing," Cassie said.

"You just want to go back for your first anniversary." Her brother elbowed her.

"And your sister gets whatever she wants," Jason smiled at his wife.

~

MARGIE PULLED THE SCARF Chaz had given her as a Christmas gift around her shoulders and rubbed it against her cheek. She would cherish the thoughtful gift and wear it often while they were apart to keep him close in the only way she could.

She snagged a Christmas cookie from the dessert spread the Reynolds' had displayed on their buffet table. The food all looked so good, but the presentation was even better. She'd never had the gift Connie had of being able to make everything look so fabulous. The rest of the company was in the other room playing Pictionary, but she'd escaped for a moment of solitude. She was an extrovert, but tonight was too much interaction even for her. Someone moved behind her, and she jumped. Chaz wrapped his arms around her waist and pulled her back against his chest. "You look beautiful tonight."

"I look tired."

"And gorgeous."

He kissed behind her ear and delightful little shivers ran all the way down to her toes. "What do you say we get out of here?"

"Sounds like music to my ears," she said. "Should we say our goodbyes?"

"It'll be easier to escape if we don't, and they'll figure out we left soon enough." He grabbed their jackets off the coat tree and helped her into hers. Casey spotted them sneaking out and gave a little wave and a conspiratorial wink.

When they reached the lodge, Chaz parked and turned in his seat to face her, taking her hands in his. "I would've brought you back to my place, but I think as tired as we both are, our inhibitions are bound to be lower than usual, so I don't trust myself to be alone with you."

She smiled and tilted her head to the side. "Good call."

"Do you mind if I come in for a little while?"

"I'd love it if you did."

He disappeared into the lodge's kitchen while she took a seat by the fireplace. He returned with a mug of hot apple cider for each of them.

"Thank you," she said.

"My pleasure."

"I have something for you. It's nothing really, but I made it for you." She stood.

"Don't discount it then." He smiled. "If you made it, then I'm sure I'll love it."

She walked over to the tree where many of the guests had placed their gifts. There weren't too many left wrapped, so it was easy to find the one she was looking for. She grabbed a box about the size of a coffee cup and brought it over to Chaz.

He took the box from her outstretched hands. "I don't have anything to give you."

"You already gave me my gifts."

"The scarf was kind of boring."

"I adore it," she said. "I love how soft it is."

He ripped into the paper, tore open the box, and pulled out the ornament with their initials and the year. "You made me an ornament?"

"It can commemorate our first Christmas together."

"We can start a memory tree like my brother's family has."

"That's the idea. But what happens after I go home? I know you're talking about looking at the chalet I have listed, but don't you think it's too soon to be talking about that? Should we be trying to find a way to make our relationship work long distance at least in the short-term?"

"I don't know, Margie. The idea of moving back to Freedom might seem sudden, but I'm afraid if we live hours away from each other, we'll drift apart."

"Maybe that would mean we weren't meant to be in the first place."

"Do you believe that?"

"I don't trust myself to know what is and isn't a good idea. I actually entertained the idea of finding a job here and abandoning my life there."

"Why, when you knew I was willing to come to you?"

"Because you shouldn't have to, Chaz." She took a long

sip of her cider and set it on the table. "You belong here. This life. Your brother's ranch. Your property in the mountains. It's you. You're more alive here then you ever were running Freedom Mountaineering."

"You didn't even know me well then. We worked together a few times when I was buying properties, but you didn't see me living my life."

"Maybe not, but I can clearly see the difference."

"We don't have to decide the future tonight," Chaz said.

She sighed. "No, I guess we don't."

"Why don't we read the Christmas story in Luke?"

"Good idea. We can end our evening with a reminder of the reason we're celebrating in the first place. I didn't bring my Bible with me, but I can go grab my Kindle."

"No need. Barry and Connie keep a few Bibles in the bookcases for guests." He pulled out a King James Bible and read aloud. The sound of his voice soothed her, and she wondered again if the chance was worth taking. Could they enjoy their twilight years together without making a mess of them?

≈

CHAZ PULLED HIS CELL out of his pocket and set it on the counter. It buzzed, jarring his already frayed nerves. He silenced it and answered. "Milo, what do you have for me?"

"Something odd is going on. I couldn't find anything on the attack itself, but I checked out the dates and times you asked me to review. I found a small-time local drug dealer, Corbin Kelly, hanging around on all those dates, but he wasn't alone. He had another guy with him. I get the feeling from the footage the other guy is in charge. If I had to guess, these guys are responsible for what happened to Kyle Shepherd."

"Thanks for looking into this." He sucked in a sharp breath and willed himself to give up control and trust Milo to take the reins. "Would you mind passing what you found along to Officer Lockhart? He drew the short straw and got called to the hospital last night. I don't know who they'll put in charge of the investigation, but he should know."

"Sure thing. I'll call the non-emergency number and see who's working tonight and give them the update if that works for you."

"That's a great idea."

"If Graham Lockhart isn't working, I'll get in touch with him in the morning to make sure he got the message. Will that work?"

"Definitely. No reason to bother him with this tonight if he's off the clock. I'm just sorry you were stuck working the holiday."

"Don't be. I don't mind the work, and security isn't a Monday-through-Friday kind of job."

"No, I guess it isn't. Merry Christmas, Milo."

"Merry Christmas."

MARGIE UNPLUGGED HER KINDLE and took it with her.

It was about time she enjoyed the jacuzzi bathtub her room provided. Her sore muscles could use the soak.

Twenty minutes later, she'd just finished dressing for bed when a knock came on her door. She cracked it open and found Casey there. "Come in, honey."

"I figured you were in the shower when you didn't answer my text a little while ago," Casey said as she plopped down on the bottom of the bed.

"Took a bath, and it was wonderful."

"That's an excellent idea. I may just take one myself. It's been a couple of years since I last had a long soak."

"Did you have a nice Christmas?" Margie asked.

"I did, but I'm worried about the villagers. Not just our church family, but all of them."

"You never did tell me what was happening that made your sending agency recall you."

"Propaganda videos came out of another missionary couple being beheaded and several villages near ours were burned to the ground by Islamic militants. They're claiming it's to rid the area of westerners spouting their religious ideas." Casey put her head in her hands. "I feel like we're giving them what they want by leaving. It's like giving in to the evil oppressors."

"Maybe, but you'll do more good alive than dead. How will you share the gospel from the grave?"

"Look at the life of Jim Elliot and the others like him. Many have been converted because of their deaths."

"I can't argue with that, but it doesn't mean you need to walk right up to the killers and give them your throat to slice. If God makes you a martyr, that's one thing, but don't go looking for it."

"I won't. Especially now." She placed her hand on her abdomen where a little baby bump was starting to show.

"I know you have mixed feelings about returning, but I'm glad you're home, and I can't wait for my grandchild to be born."

"I've missed you, Mom." Casey gave her a hug. "I better get back in there before Gage sends out a search party. Merry Christmas."

"Merry Christmas, sweetheart."

CHAPTER 17

CHAZ SAT IN THE wooden rocking chair on his porch, sipping his coffee as he watched the sunrise Thursday morning. A dusting of snow covered the hills in the distance, and there was a bite in the air. He drank the last sip of lukewarm coffee and stood. There was much to be done and little time left to do it. First stop, the ranch office.

As he neared the office, he spotted Leona leaning against the post-and-rail fence, gazing out over the pastures.

"Hey. How's it going?" he asked. "Enjoying your stay?"

"It's nice, but it'd be better if you weren't so distracted all the time. I've hardly seen you since the camping trip."

He was certain he'd seen her a number of times since then, but maybe he could've been friendlier. He had a tendency to withdraw inside himself sometimes. "Sorry. I've been distracted."

"She's an attractive distraction." She laughed. "A little young for you though."

He shrugged. This wasn't a topic he was comfortable talking about with his high-school girlfriend. They hadn't been close in a long time, and he had no interest in going back in time.

"Did you enjoy your visit with Connie the other day?"

She looked puzzled, so he let it drop. "I've got to head in there, but I'll see you around."

When he entered, Barry was going over something with Cassie and gestured for him to sit and wait for a few minutes. He tried, but restless energy had him on his feet again within seconds.

Cassie laughed. "Let's continue this later. I think Uncle Chaz needs a minute of your time."

"Actually, I need to talk to both of you."

He removed his cowboy hat and ran the sleeve of his flannel shirt over his forehead to dry the perspiration. No reason for sweating when it was freezing outside. "What do you have the temperature set to in here? Eighty-three?"

"Sixty-eight. You okay?" Cassie asked.

"Fine. Yeah. I'm thinking about moving back to Freedom Ridge."

"Is this about Margie?" Barry asked.

"Maybe I should go," Cassie said.

"Stay. I'm giving my notice. You need to know that more than your dad. You make the schedules."

"I'm sure that mission that gets your paychecks won't be too happy," Barry said.

"They'll survive without the pittance I send their way."

"Don't you think you should give it some time and make sure this is really what you both want? It feels like you're rushing into this." Barry turned to Cassie with a look that said 'talk some sense into your uncle.'

She shook her head. "If you're sure, you're sure. Most people would say Jason and I jumped into things, but I'm glad we did."

"You're not helping, Cass."

"Sorry, Dad." She gave Chaz a hug. "If you love her, don't let her go."

~

MARGIE HESITATED IN FRONT of the real estate office in downtown Redemption. She would just feel them out. Today didn't have to be the day for making life-altering decisions. If God opened a door, she would walk through it, but first she had to be sure it was His will. Lifting up a prayer, she pushed the door open and ambled inside.

"May I help you?"

"I hope so. I'm Margie Crawford. I spoke with someone on the phone about a job."

"Great to meet you, Margie. I'm Bertha, the secretary, receptionist, and all-around gal Friday."

Margie couldn't help but smile. "Nice to meet you."

"Wendy will be with you in a minute. She's so excited that you're thinking about joining us. I think she seriously considered baking you a cake, but she was afraid it would be too much too soon."

They were supposed to be interviewing her for a position, but they made it sound like it was the other way around. Maybe it was. She needed to make sure it was a good fit before leaving the job she'd held since shortly after graduating high school.

An hour later, she left the office feeling good about the

possibility. If Chaz genuinely wanted them to be together, then they could do so here in his hometown. She didn't have the family connections in Freedom that he had here. This was where he belonged, so if he wanted her by his side, this would be the place for them. She had no intention of living on the ranch though. They'd either need to consider building on his land or buying a place.

On the return drive, she weighed the pros and cons of taking the job or turning it down. She prayed for answers and when she looked up, she noticed a car following too closely. She took a left turn, and the car turned with her. Maybe they were going to the ranch, too. She slowed to pull over and let the car pass, but it slowed and pulled behind her. She sped away and made several turns until she lost the other vehicle. It was one time she was grateful for having been married to a police officer who taught her how to lose a tail. Trying to tell herself it was nothing and she was imagining things wasn't working. Her hands shook on the wheel as she drove back to the ranch.

∽

CHAZ WALTZED INTO THE lodge looking for Margie. He hoped to convince her to have dinner with him. He wanted to get her alone and ask her to attend the charity concert at the Mesa with him. It wasn't really his kind of thing. He preferred quieter pursuits these days, but if he was going to ask the woman to spend the rest of her life with him, he needed to put a little thought into the proposal.

After checking the common areas, he went up to her room. At his knock, she opened the door with a smile. "I wasn't expecting you. Come on in."

A light floral scent lingered on her skin, and he drank it in as she hugged him. Yes, he was absolutely sure that he wanted that experience every day for the rest of his life. When she drew back, he cradled her face with his hands and moved in for a lingering kiss. When he pulled back, he looked into her eyes. "I was hoping you'd agree to have dinner with me."

"Connie called a few minutes ago. She and Barry had tickets for the dinner theater tonight, and they can't make it. It's called *The Silent Night Conspiracy*. Interested?"

"Well, I was going to take you to the fast-food joint for burgers and fries, but I suppose I'll settle for steak."

"There isn't a fast-food place within thirty miles of here."

"Maybe that was the point. I wanted you trapped in the car with me for a longer time."

She laughed, and he reveled in the sound.

"Before we get going, do you want to attend the charity concert at the Mesa with me New Year's Eve?"

Nodding, she said, "Sounds like a nice way to ring in the new year."

MARGIE SPENT THE NEXT three hours trying to solve the mystery along with the characters in the play. The ending came out of nowhere, but looking back she realized the answers had been woven throughout the story in a masterful way that didn't give away the ending. One thing was certain: She needed to return to see their next production because *The Silent Night Conspiracy* was riveting, and she longed to see the cast's versatility. It was her understanding, they performed comedies and tragedies as well as mysteries. She couldn't imagine the talent they must have to be able to do that.

Chaz threaded his fingers with hers as they walked back to the car. She noticed Leona standing afar off, and almost suggested that they go chat with her. Maybe Chaz' presence would ease the dislike the woman seemed to have for her. Changing her mind about talking to the disagreeable woman, she leaned into Chaz' side, drawing strength from him. "Tonight was fun."

"It was. We should do this again soon." The words he spoke held a weight, and she knew he was questioning whether their relationship would survive the next few weeks or not. A few days ago, she had her doubts, but she was coming to accept that life was short, and they needed to make the most of it.

"How does dessert sound? I don't feel like taking you home quite yet."

"We just ate dessert."

"That tiny slice of cheesecake? That doesn't count."

"What did you have in mind?" she asked.

"How about a big old slice of apple pie with vanilla ice cream?"

"Sounds good. Where will we get it?"

"Flapjacks, of course."

She smiled as he opened the passenger door for her. As he headed back to town, she caught sight of a vehicle trailing too close and her mind snapped back to the car following her on her way home, but she brushed the memory aside. It might be nothing, and Chaz didn't need to be bothered with her imaginations.

CHAPTER 18

MARGIE TOOK A SEAT where indicated and smiled at the woman who sat down across from her. "What did you want to have done today?"

"Need a manicure. Had one several weeks ago at Redemption Spa, but my nails have grown, so there is a gap, and the paint is chipping."

"Let me see those." She lifted her hand. "Not bad for a few weeks of wear and tear over at the ranch." The woman raised an eyebrow.

"Yes. I'm staying at the ranch. Decided to spend the holidays here and have a bit of adventure."

"That sounds nice. I'm Lottie, by the way."

"Nice to meet you. I'm Margie."

"You want to go with a similar color or something festive?"

"What are you thinking?" Margie asked.

"New Year's Eve is coming up, so how about a gold color and maybe some nail art?"

"I think I might like gold. What kind of nail art?"

"We could do hearts or stars, or a combination of both?"

"I don't know. I'm afraid they'd be gaudy."

Lottie laughed. "I don't do gaudy. They'll be lovely."

"Okay. I'll give it a try." She shrugged. "What do I have to lose?"

"So, what are your plans for the holiday?"

"We're going to the charity concert at the Mesa."

"Who is 'we'?"

"Me and Chaz. He's my daughter's father-in-law." Her face grew warm, and she knew she was turning red. Sometimes she really wanted to curse her Scandinavian complexion.

"Oh, I know who Chaz is. I was in junior high when he graduated high school, but all the girls knew the rodeo champion."

"I've always known him as a businessman. Seeing him here in his element changed my perception of him."

"I can see that by the healthy blush on your cheeks. What happens when you go home?"

Margie glanced around the room to make sure nobody else was listening. "I may not go home. I'm a real estate agent, and I interviewed here in town. They offered me a job. I have to take the time to think it over, but I might take it."

"Wow. That's wonderful. Congratulations, and welcome to Redemption."

"I didn't take the job."

"Not yet, but you will."

They continued to chat like old friends while Lottie pushed back her cuticles, filed her nails, and painted them a classy gold color. The tiny silver hearts and stars she adorned them with turned out to be classy rather than tacky and

Margie was glad she'd decided to accept the suggestion.

The door to the salon banged shut when she exited, and she cringed, wishing she'd have held it until it closed. As she headed to her car, someone came out of the shadows. She pulled the can of mace from her pocket. It was one thing she didn't leave home without since her abduction a couple years prior. Whoever it was she'd seen must've moved along since she didn't see them anymore. She climbed into her car and let out a shaky breath. Then she saw it. Someone had gotten into her vehicle and secured a note to the passenger seat with a camouflage hunting knife. She shrieked and several heads turned toward her. Knowing she shouldn't touch the handle since it might have prints on it, she tried to read around the knife while she hyperventilated. "Go home!" The letters pasted to the page had been cut out from a newspaper. With shaky hands she dialed 911 and reported the incident.

⁓

CHAZ FINISHED POPPING ON the LockJawz to secure a piece of fence, then fished his phone out of his back pocket. It had been buzzing for the past ten minutes, but he'd been occupied with daily tasks and hadn't had time to check and see who was texting.

Several were from an unknown number and listed as potential spam, so he deleted them without wasting his time reading. Then he came to one from Milo asking him to stop by the security office. He checked the time and decided to stop for the day. He'd shower and then head to the lodge. After he talked with Milo, he'd check and see if Margie was around. Hopefully, she wasn't sick of seeing him.

When he sauntered into the lodge a short time later, he saw Margie sitting at a table with Leticia. He stopped at the table, put his hands on her shoulders, and bent down to give her a kiss on the cheek. "I have to stop in at the security office, but I was wondering if you might want to spend some time together tonight."

She smiled, but there was an underlying tension beneath it. Something was wrong. "Sure. That'd be nice."

"You okay?"

"We can talk about it later."

"Did I do something wrong?"

"No, Chaz. We're good."

He walked away with a distinct sense of loss. Was she planning to end their relationship? Sure seemed like it to him. He let himself into the security office and dropped into one of the chairs. One of the screens showed Margie and Leticia still at the table where he'd left them, but Margie had crossed her arms on the table and rested her head on them. He felt her weariness and wondered at the cause.

Milo swiveled around to face him. "You all right?"

"I will be. What do you have for me?"

"Officer Hughes and I are friends, so I called in a favor and got us some information that won't be made public."

"What's that?"

"Kyle owed some pretty rough guys some money for drugs they gave him. Turns out he paid with counterfeit bills, and when they tried to pass them, they learned that they'd been duped."

"I wouldn't imagine it's a smart move to try to cheat your dealer."

"No. I'm sure he's learned his lesson about that. Hopefully, he's learned his lesson all around and cleans up his act."

"So, what are you telling me? He was stealing from the ranch to pay back the drug dealers?"

"That's what it looks like."

"Then why did they beat him and leave him for dead?"

"They requested a 'favor' to pay them back what he still owed. He didn't deliver."

"What was the favor?"

"They wanted him to scare off one of our guests."

"Which one?"

"Margie Crawford."

～

CHAZ RETURNED TO THE dining room, and Margie gave Leticia a weak smile. "Guess it's time to tell him about what happened in town."

"You need me to tell him what you told me?" Leticia asked. "You've had a hard day. Maybe you should just head on upstairs and rest."

She shook her head. "Thanks for the offer, but he deserves to hear it from me."

Chaz approached the table. "Snow's coming down hard out there, mind grabbing your coat and snow boots? I'd prefer to talk at my place where we have more privacy."

Sucking in a sharp breath, she nodded. "I'll be right back." She could invite him upstairs to talk in her living area, but the quarters were too close for comfort especially when she was feeling needy and desperate. It probably wasn't the best idea to head to his house either, but she agreed with him that they needed privacy for the discussion they were about to have. She needed to tell him what happened, and she hoped he wouldn't decide he wanted nothing more to do with her and her problems.

When she returned, she found him waiting by the door. "Ready?"

She nodded.

They were silent on the walk from the lodge to his house. "Give me a few minutes to start a fire. Then we can talk."

Curling her legs up under her, she pulled the fleece blanket from the back of his couch and covered herself with it. It offered some measure of comfort, but her stomach remained in knots. When the fire was blazing, Chaz took the seat beside her on the couch. "Today has been enlightening."

"In what way?"

"We'll get to that in a minute. First, what was bothering you when I got to the lodge? I had the distinct impression you were ready to tell me you were ready to dump me."

"No. Nothing like that." She shook her head, pulled out her phone, brought up a photo of the knife from her camera roll and handed it to him.

"When did this happen?" he asked.

"Today when I was leaving the nail salon in town."

"Why didn't you call me? I would've come right out."

"I probably should've." She traced a heart on the nail of her ring finger. "But I'm used to dealing with things on my own."

"You know I would've wanted to be there for you."

She swallowed hard. "I called the police."

"What did they say?"

"Not much. They took the knife and the note in for evidence and said they would check surveillance cameras from the local businesses to see if any of them caught someone going into my car."

"Let's hope they did."

"This is probably connected to my ex. You remember what happened to me and Casey a couple of years back. This is likely more of the same. I don't think it's safe for me to stay here. I could be putting you and the rest of your family in danger simply by being on the property."

"Whoever is threatening you will be dealt with, but don't let them chase you away. Even if you and I weren't involved, you're my son's mother-in-law. That makes you family, too. Family bands together. We don't send one member off to deal with unknown threats alone."

"But I'd never forgive myself if I were the cause of something happening to someone you loved."

He lifted her chin, so she was forced to look into his eyes. "What if that someone was you? If you run off, you're putting yourself in danger."

It wasn't lost on her that he'd just told her he loved her, but she wasn't sure how to respond. What he was asking wasn't easy. He wanted her to risk putting him in harm's way. She wasn't sure she could do that.

Chaz pulled her close and kissed the top of her head. The gesture was comforting and made her long to stay with him. To trust her future to him.

~

MARGIE INCHED AWAY FROM him and drew in a ragged breath. "You never told me what was enlightening about today."

He felt her drawing back again, and it frustrated him. If they were going to be together, he needed her to trust him to keep her safe. But she wouldn't even trust him with her heart. She hadn't told him she loved him, and he'd given her the opening to do so. Unless he was reading her wrong, the same emotions raging inside him were alive in her, too, but he couldn't be certain unless she shared how she felt.

"Are you going to tell me what happened in the security office or not?" She scooted back, putting distance between them on the couch.

"Milo had an update on why Kyle took that beating."

"And why was that?"

"You sure you want to know?"

She nodded. "I do."

"Because he wouldn't do something to scare you enough to make you run back home."

"Something like the knife through my passenger seat."

"Maybe." He was afraid they'd wanted Kyle to do more than leave a threatening note, but there was no reason to frighten her any more than she already was.

"What do they want with me?"

He shook his head. That was where he was lost. "I'm hoping the cops can find out."

"How did Kyle get involved with those people in the first place?"

Chaz broke down the story as he'd heard it, and then reached for her again. "Are you going to let me hold you, or are you going to continue to keep three feet between us for the remainder of the evening?"

"I haven't decided."

He scooted to her side of the couch. "How about if I decide for you? Would that be all right with you?"

At her nod, he drew her into his arms and lowered his lips to within an inch of hers, but before he kissed her, he whispered, "I love you, Margie. Don't make any rash decisions tonight, please."

She didn't answer, but she wrapped her arms around his neck and pulled his lips down to meet hers. "Just kiss me."

CHAPTER 19

CHAZ WALKED HER TO the door of the lodge. "I'd come up with you, but it's probably best if I don't."

The corners of her lips lifted, and she leaned in for a hug. "I'll see you at church?"

He nodded. "I'll be there. Goodnight, Margie." After one last lingering kiss, he left, and she heard Leticia shouting from the other room. "I done saw that. Don't be trying to tell me he's just your daughter's father-in-law anymore."

Margie let out a giggle. If she could take him at his word, he loved her. She'd trusted those words when John had spoken them, and it had burned her in the end. Not that she regretted her marriage. If it weren't for John she wouldn't have Casey, and Casey meant everything to her. But she found it difficult to take the words at face value. Chaz had shown her how he felt though. Repeatedly since she'd arrived on the ranch, he'd put her needs ahead of his own. There was no good reason for her to doubt him. And she did love him. The depth of feeling burning inside her for him was unmistakable and undeniable. He'd burrowed into her heart, and there was no way she was going to get him out now.

"Yes, Leticia. You're right. He is far more than that."

"Come over here and tell me all about it."

She smiled. "Maybe tomorrow. Right now, I need to get some sleep."

When she reached her room, the door was ajar. She was certain she hadn't left it that way. She'd given Casey a key card, maybe she was inside. Pushing the door a little farther open she called, "Case?"

"No. It's me." A woman pushed the door closed with her foot as she wrapped her elbow around Margie's throat, cutting off her oxygen. "Can't let you scream now, can I?"

The voice was familiar, but she hadn't yet gotten a good look at the woman. She let some of the pressure off and Margie screamed, but the sound was cut off when duct tape was secured across her mouth. She kicked and clawed but couldn't get good leverage.

"Hold still." The woman wound the duct tape around her wrists and pulled her to the bed. "Sit down and I won't have to hurt you. I don't want to kill you, but I will if I must."

That's when Margie realized it was Leona. And she held a knife to her throat. Margie's eyes widened, but she couldn't speak with her mouth covered.

"Why didn't you stay in Freedom Ridge? I had those gang bangers go mess up one of your properties to get you to run back to your job. You should've stayed there. You aren't wanted here." Leona let out a bitter laugh. "I can see your confusion. Let me clear it up for you. Chaz loves me, and I love him. We were together all the way back in high school, you know? He was the first guy who held my hand. The first one who kissed me. Then he met that tramp, Suzanne, and married her.

"Well, he finally returned to Redemption and to me, and I planned my time off work so I could be here on the ranch and remind him of what we'd had together, but you had to waltz your skinny self in here and try to take him from me. I won't have it. No. He's mine, so you're going to head back where you came from, or I'm going to bury you so far out on the range that nobody will ever find your body." She moved in close, so her face was inches from Margie's. "Or maybe I'll toss you over one of our many majestic cliffs. Are we clear?"

Margie nodded, but the woman didn't remove the bindings. Instead, she dragged her from the bed to the rocking chair by the window and tied her to it. "This should keep you out of the way until I can figure out how to get you out of town without drawing attention to myself. Don't do anything stupid while I'm away."

∾

WHEN SERVICE WAS OVER, instead of joining the potluck dinner, Chaz headed back to the lodge. Margie had agreed to come to service, but she hadn't followed through. He needed to find out what was going on inside her head before she did something stupid like trying to investigate the threat herself or heading back to Freedom Ridge before he could propose. If she did that, he'd follow her. He knew that much, but he'd prefer she agreed to be his wife before he moved back.

He pushed open the door of the lodge with more force than necessary. Seeing Casey and Gage in the dining room, he hurried over. "Why weren't you two at service?"

"Casey wanted to check out the Triple R Chapel, so we went there." Gage frowned. "Why do you look like you're ready to tear this place apart stone by stone?"

"Margie didn't show up to service. I'm not sure what is going on in that woman's head."

"Mom has a strong will, but it's crystal clear how she feels about you. Give her time to come to grips with her emotions."

"Would you mind going upstairs and asking her to come down? I need to see for myself that she hasn't headed back to Freedom."

"She wouldn't leave without saying goodbye."

"Please check." His hands were fisted at his sides, and he forced them to relax.

Gage put a hand on his shoulder. "Let's sit by the fire. You need to take some deep breaths and say a prayer or two before she comes down here. You're far too wired to see her right now."

"You're right. That woman will be the death of me. She drives me crazy, but I can't imagine letting her go."

"I get that. Her daughter is the same way."

Casey called to them, and they turned to find her halfway down the stairs. "You two need to come up here."

Chaz stood in the doorway of Margie's room. Duct tape clung to the chair, and more was crumpled on the floor. Blood. It wasn't a lot, but it was enough to send tendrils of fear up his spine. "Lord, please keep her safe." He dialed 911.

Casey sank down on the edge of the bed. "This can't be happening again. I can't go through this again."

Gage kissed the top of his wife's head. "We'll get through this the same as we got through it the first time."

"But Brim's in prison. Supposed to be serving another ten years. Who could've taken my mom this time?" Her tear-filled eyes settled on Chaz. "Do you have any idea who could have her?"

"No, but I'm hoping the cops will. They knew there had been threats against her."

"Threats? She didn't say anything."

"Probably didn't have a chance. She only found out yesterday. Let's wait for the police downstairs. We shouldn't mess up the scene." Chaz gestured to the door.

∽

MARGIE'S HEAD WAS TOO heavy to lift, and she couldn't move her hands and feet. Rustling nearby told her she wasn't alone. Her cheek rested on rough boards. Mold and mildew choked off her airways, making it a struggle to get a full breath.

Then she remembered. Leona. She'd returned to her room with a needle. She didn't know what she'd been dosed with, but apparently it had a paralytic effect. Closing her eyes, she begged God to help her find a way out of this. When she next opened them, her kidnapper stood sneering down at her.

"What am I supposed to do with you? Huh? I can't just let you go. You'll go to the police. Or worse, you'll run to Chaz and cry on his shoulder telling how awful I was. That won't do me any favors.

"You could disappear. That would be for the best. I hadn't planned to kill you. I just wanted you out of the way, but I wasn't thinking. This is all your fault. If you had just stayed away from here, none of this would've happened. You shouldn't have come to Redemption Ridge."

The kick Leona delivered to her ribs before storming out, should've hurt, but Margie couldn't feel a thing.

⁓

CHAZ STARED AT THE dying embers in the fireplace as he silently begged God to keep Margie safe. He jumped at a tap on his shoulder.

"Sorry, didn't mean to startle you," Officer Graham Lockhart said.

"So, what happens next? Are you going to go look for her?"

"We got a lead on Kyle's beating, so we're hoping it might lead to whoever abducted Ms. Crawford."

"What's the lead?"

"I can't share that with you. We don't need civilians making it impossible for us to do our jobs."

Chaz frowned and turned away from the cop. He'd find a way to get the information he needed, so he could start searching for Margie. Milo might know something. Moments later, he let himself into the security room and pierced Milo with a stare. "Lockhart said something about a lead. I know about Corbin Kelly, but did we find out who the other guy on the footage was?"

"It was Tony Marte. He thinks he's some kind of gangster, but he's nothing more than a wannabe."

"Do you think he has Margie?"

"Doubt it, but he might know who does."

"Where can I find him?"

"It's not a good idea for you to go there, Chaz. You might end up getting yourself shot."

"I'm not worried about myself right now. Margie needs me, and I won't sit on my hands and do nothing."

Milo scrawled something down on a scrap of paper and handed it to him. "A bar?"

"He dabbles in many pursuits, but taking bets is one of them."

"The kid's a bookie?"

"Yeah."

"I thought they were obsolete now that it's so easy to place bets online."

"You'd think that, wouldn't you?" Milo stood. "I guess as long as they have customers, they'll keep taking wagers."

"If Gage is looking for me later, don't tell him where I went."

"No promises."

Chaz shook his head and stormed out. He could be at Dino's Sports Bar in less than fifteen minutes.

CHAPTER 20

THE FEELING IN MARGIE'S arms and legs slowly returned. Leona had been gone for some time. She wasn't quite sure how long, but it felt like hours. As jumpy as her abductor seemed when she'd awakened earlier, she was afraid in her desperation, she might do what she'd threatened. Which meant Margie needed to get herself to safety before the other woman returned to finish her off.

Her hands and feet were bound, and she'd been left on the floor. She forced herself to rise to a seated position and scooted until her back was against the slatted wall of a ramshackle barn. The strength it took to move sapped most of her energy, but it was imperative that she keep going. Inch by inch, she slid along the wall until she reached what looked like an old workbench. There were tools on it. Probably rusted and useless, but she might find something to help rid her of the duct tape. She forced herself to her feet and tried to find something that might help her. There was an old, rusted wrench as well as a hammer that might help if she could use the claw to saw through the tape, but it would be hard to do with her hands tied behind her. A creaking sound reached her so she backed up to the table, grabbing whatever she could before the opportunity passed. Then she ducked under a nearby tarp that she soon learned covered an ancient tractor.

"Yoohoo? Where did you run off to, Margie?" The woman giggled. "I'm sure you aren't running anywhere with your legs duct-taped and the ketamine slowing your reflexes, so where oh where can you be?"

Margie listened as her abductor searched for her. It was only a matter of time until she found her.

∽

Chaz reached Dino's Sports Bar in record time, but there were two Redemption Ridge Police Department cruisers parked outside. He was fairly certain that between them and the two at the ranch, they'd exhausted the resources of the local police. Which meant nobody was out searching for Margie. He stepped inside and took a moment to allow his eyes to adjust to the dark interior. Then he sidled up to the bar as close to the cops as he could get without being noticed and ordered a coke. The bartender raised a brow, but he ignored the unspoken question and listened to the interview taking place ten feet from his barstool.

He looked over his shoulder to study the kid the cops were questioning. If he were to describe him in one word, he'd use the word smarmy. A cop slammed his hand on the table, and their interviewee jumped back, taking his chair with him. "Give me a name!"

"I ain't giving you no names. You trying to get me

killed?"

"A woman is missing, and if you don't give me something, I'm pinning her disappearance on you."

"I didn't kidnap no woman."

"You're as good a suspect as any. Who asked you to hurt the woman?"

"I never hurt her, so it don't matter."

"But you did send your minions to harm Kyle when he wouldn't take care of the lady, didn't you?"

"I didn't lay a hand on the kid myself."

"Let's lock him in a cell and see if he comes to his senses."

"We should have enough to hold him now that the thugs he paid to give Kyle that beat down are talking."

"Ain't nobody talking to you."

"Want to put your bets on that, bookie?"

"Fine. I'll give you her first name. That's all I have."

"What is it?"

"Leona."

The blood drained from Chaz' face, and he steadied himself on the bar to keep from falling over. Why on earth would Leona want to hurt Margie? Then memories came back unbidden. A kiss after the rodeo. A few nights hanging out under the stars. Some horseback rides in the moonlight. His family's ranch was next to the Chambers' family ranch. They were childhood friends. And a little bit more. She was angry when he'd brought Suzanne home, but that was a lifetime ago. Surely, she'd moved on. Was it possible she was still obsessing over a relationship from high school? He swallowed the lump in his throat. It explained everything. How he'd been seeing her everywhere on the ranch. The weird conversation they'd had when he saw her leaving his brother's driveway. All the time she spent hanging out in the barn when he was there. He'd figured she just loved spending time with the horses. It never occurred to him that she was trying to get his attention.

He flew from the bar, jumped in his car, and headed up the mountain. The first place to look was back where it all started.

~

Margie hid inside the wheel of the enormous tractor and fingered the handful of items she'd managed to snag from the workbench, trying to figure out what she'd pilfered. One of the pieces of metal felt like a hinge. It had a ragged edge where it must've rusted through. If she could position it right, she might be able to use it to saw through the duct tape. Keeping her breathing even so Leona wouldn't find her, she attempted to free herself.

"This game is getting old. Where are you?" Leona whistled to the tune of "There was a Farmer, Had a Dog," but then she stopped whistling and sang in a singsong voice, "There was a farmer, had a tramp. Here a squeak, there a clunk, everywhere a squeak, clunk."

The footsteps moved closer, and Margie bit down on her lip, tasting her own blood.

The tarp was torn off the tractor, and her tormentor grinned down at her. "Did you really think you could hide from me?" The woman had a rifle gripped in her hands.

"Let's go. I don't want to make a mess in the barn. We'll take a short walk."

Margie knew she wouldn't be able to continue working the duct tape if Leona was following her with a gun. Was this how it would end? After surviving all that time in the earth when Brim tossed her into his animal trap, would she die at the hands of the jealous ex-girlfriend of the man she loved?

～

CHAZ DROVE DOWN THE long drive to his family's old ranch. It was only one week ago that he'd brought Margie here to cut a Christmas tree. He refused to allow it to be the last time. She was here somewhere. Either here or on the Chambers' property. He parked and went inside the dilapidated house. It hadn't been touched since his mother abandoned it so long ago. Thick dust covered the blankets draped over the furniture. He wasn't sure his father's old shotgun would still be there. But the last time he'd been inside, everything was as they'd left it, so he hoped for the best.

If he showed up to save Margie unarmed, he wouldn't stand much of a chance against an obsessed ranch woman. Especially if she had a gun, and he imagined she did.

In his parents' bedroom closet, he found it. The safe was locked, but it was right where he was hoping it would be. His father had kept the key in his nightstand. Probably not the most secure choice, but at least the weapon was locked up. Chaz pulled the blanket off it, and something skittered across the floor. Stepping back, he took another deep breath before pulling open the nightstand drawer. In an old film canister, right where he remembered his father keeping them, he found the keys to the safe.

Inside it, he found the shotgun and enough shells to wipe out Colorado's entire population of deer.

He scoped out the path between his property and the Chambers' ranch. They'd worn it down as kids, but it was overgrown now. His footsteps crunched in the frozen snow as he headed toward the old silo where Leona had professed her feelings for him. He looked inside and bellowed for Margie, but only echoes answered his call.

~

MARGIE TENSED WHEN SHE heard Chaz' voice echoing off the hills.

"Don't go thinking he's going to rescue you. He may think he's here to save you, but once he sees that you're dead, he'll come to his senses and realize I was the one he belonged with all along."

It didn't seem like the right time to remind Leona that she was very much alive, so she started working on the duct tape again while her captor kept watch over her shoulder. A sharp drop-off up ahead gave her a clue as to Leona's plans for her. A single shot and she'd tumble down the hill never to be seen again. That might present a problem though when Chaz heard the gunshot and called the police. Why weren't the cops here? If he'd come, surely, he would've alerted them of the location. Unless they were awaiting a warrant. In which case, she appreciated his reckless disregard for their rules. He might be just the distraction she needed. The cliff loomed ahead, and she swallowed hard and tugged until the last bit of duct tape tore and her hands were free. An inhuman sound came from Leona as Margie turned and kicked the rifle. A deafening shot split the air as Margie tackled the other woman, landing a blow in her gut and then another to her face. She wrestled the weapon from her and used her shoulder to steady it. "On your feet."

The sound of footfalls running toward them snapped her head up, and Leona used the momentary distraction to attack her again and try to gain control of the weapon, but Margie held tight. The sight of Chaz on the path brought a hint of a smile to her lips. "I could use a little help over here," she said.

His gaze raked over her, and she knew he was taking inventory to see if she was injured and needed medical attention. "I'm fine. Just take her off my hands. I don't want to have to look at her any longer."

He tossed Margie his cell phone. "Keep trying to get service. You should manage to get a bar or two once we get over the ridge. I want the cops to come collect her."

"Let's go," Chaz directed the comment to Leona who looked back at him with a pitiful expression. Margie almost felt sorry for her. Almost.

Chapter 21

Chaz massaged Margie's shoulders as she answered yet another question from the detective. Three hours had passed since they'd arrived at the hospital, and it was past time for them to let her rest.

Chaz gave him a pointed look, and the detective whose name Chaz had forgotten already, stood and leaned his weight against the doorway. "We'll have more questions for you later, but it's getting late, so you should get some rest." He tapped the door frame twice and disappeared down the hall.

"When can I get out of here?" Margie gave Chaz a weak smile.

"Soon, I think."

"I hope so, otherwise I won't have time to rest up and get ready for our date tomorrow night."

"You still want to go after all you've been through? Don't you need time to recover?"

"One thing this ordeal taught me is that life is unpredictable and can be short, so I shouldn't take for granted the important moments, and I have a feeling tomorrow night is going to be one for the record books."

"What makes you think that?"

"Just a feeling I get."

Two hours later, they were sitting by the fire in the lodge sipping hot cocoa as Barry, Connie, Casey, Gage, and Leticia all flitted around Margie trying to make her comfortable. He'd been hoping for some time alone, but all he'd had was the few minutes in the car on the way back to the ranch.

He drank down some melted marshmallows and thought about his plans for the next night. From what Margie had said at the hospital, he assumed she knew he was planning to propose, but he could find a way to make the proposal a bit more unexpected and maybe give it some kind of twist to make it more memorable.

❧

MARGIE SMILED AS SHE slid her diamond studs into her ears. A tiny bottle of her favorite fragrance sat on the dresser, and she opened it and dabbed it behind her ears. It had a light floral scent that reminded her of a spring breeze with a hint of lilac. She planned to tell Chaz that she was going to accept the job in Redemption and move to town. He'd talked about the possibility of coming to Freedom Ridge so they could continue their courtship, but she was certain this was where they belonged despite all that had happened with Leona. Drawing in a steadying breath, she reminded herself that the woman was behind bars where she belonged. It was sad. She didn't know how someone could go from being a productive member of society to becoming a stalker and kidnapper.

But tonight, Margie's focus was on the man she loved. And tonight, she would tell him how she felt about him. No more keeping her feelings in their protective shell. It was time to risk her heart and love again.

A soft knock on her door had her double checking her makeup and hair before answering.

"Hi." His gaze roamed over her, and heat rushed to her cheeks. "You look amazing."

She grabbed the scarf he'd gotten her for Christmas that doubled as a wrap from the back of the chair and draped it over her shoulders. "I'm ready when you are."

"I think you're forgetting something."

"Nah. Left my shoes downstairs. Didn't want to chance the stairs in three-inch heels."

"You should probably ditch the high heels permanently."

"This dress would look silly with anything else."

"Nah. It would look perfect with those cowgirl boots you're so fond of wearing."

"You think?"

"I do."

She bent down and pulled the Lucchese box from under the bed, slipped on a pair of socks, and tugged the boots on. Inspecting herself in the mirror, she asked, "Are you sure these look all right?"

"You look downright adorable in them."

〜

GAGE AND CASEY HAD already held a table for them, so when they arrived at the Mesa, they joined them there. The music was too loud, and the lack of privacy a bit grating, but Chaz was determined to make sure he didn't let his preference for a calmer atmosphere ruin their special evening.

Everything was set. Barry had spoken to Mia Rose's manager for him, and he'd agreed to set it all up. Now he simply needed to wait for the song so he could proceed. Just before the end of their first set, the music slowed down and the strains of "Rockin' Years" filled the room. Margie squeezed his hand. "This was the first song we waltzed to; I can't believe she's playing it." Mia Rose had that Dolly Parton twang that brought the song to life.

Chaz handed Margie a wrapped box, and her eyes locked on his. She took a deep breath and opened it. He could see the disappointment when she saw the bracelet, but her eyes lit when she noticed the tiny rocking chair charm attached to it. Yeah. She got the message. He helped her fasten it to her wrist. When she looked back up, Gage and Casey had moved away from the table. He stood and followed them. Gage held his sign up first. It read 'Will...," then Casey lifted hers: 'you...' and Chaz raised his, 'marry me?'

Her hand flew to her mouth, and she nodded.

Margie Crawford had just agreed to be his wife. He threw down the sign and raced back to her side, lifting and spinning her. He reached into his pocket, extracted the ring, and placed it on her finger. A perfect fit, thanks to Casey who gave him her ring size.

❧

MARGIE COULDN'T STOP GRINNING the rest of the evening. She turned her hand every which way to watch the lights glint on the princess-cut diamond. It wasn't quite the way she'd expected the evening to go, but she couldn't have been happier. They said their goodbyes to Gage and Casey in the parking lot, and Chaz drove her back to the lodge.

When they parked, he turned to face her. "I know you're supposed to go home tomorrow."

"I am."

"I gave my notice last week, but it'll be another month or two before I can manage to buy a place in Freedom Ridge and get out there."

"You're not coming to Freedom."

"Of course, I am. You agreed to marry me, and we can't live in separate places."

"I took a job in Redemption. January 31st is my last day at my current job."

"Are you serious?"

"Freedom is just a town to me, Chaz. This place is in your blood, I could never ask you to leave."

"You didn't ask."

"Even without the proposal, I was going to come here and see if we could give this relationship a go. Now you've cemented it for me. I'll be back soon." She giggled. "When do you want to get married?"

"Is tonight too soon?"

Another laugh escaped. "Maybe. How about the first

173

Saturday in February?"

"That would be February 1st." He grinned. "Works for me."

∼

Ready for more?
Return to Redemption Ridge in *Dreaming about Forever* by Mandi Blake, the next book in the Christmas in Redemption Ridge series.

Her handsome bodyguard is doing a great job protecting her from reporters, but she may need to protect her heart.

∼

Join in all the fun at our Facebook Reader Group
<u>www.facebook.com/groups/freedomridgereaders</u>
For sneak peeks, giveaways, and tons of Christmas
romance fun!

Christmas in Redemption Ridge Series

View the Series Here

Year 1
Marrying the Rancher's Daughter
(Jason and Cassie)
By Tara Grace Ericson

Remembering the Rancher
(Maverick and Annabella) By Liwen Ho

Year 2
Amending the Christmas Contract
(Levi and Ruby)
By Hannah Jo Abbott

Wooing the Widower
(Chaz and Margie) By Elle E Kay

Year 3
Dreaming About Forever
(Jordan and Alicia) By Mandi Blake

Bidding on a Second Chance
(Graham and Piper)
By Emily Conrad

A CHRISTIAN ARMY RANGER CHRISTMAS ROMANCE
Persuaded by the Hero
A CHRISTIAN ARMY VETERAN CHRISTMAS ROMANCE
Inspired by the Hero
A CHRISTIAN PHYSICIAN ASSISTANT CHRISTMAS RO-
MANCE

Christmas in Redemption Ridge Series
Wooing the Widower

Pennsylvania Parks Series
Grave Pursuits
Grave Secrets
Grave Consequences

Standalone Novella
Holly's Noel

READER LETTER

Dear Reader,

I hope you enjoyed reading *Wooing the Widower*. If you did, check out some of my other titles. For a list of my current books and upcoming releases check out the novel page on my website at https://elleekay.com/novels.

I'd love it if you'd sign up for my newsletter at https://elleekay.com/newsletter-signup/, so I'll send you a free book when you do.

Go to https://books2read.com/ap/xdPqqN/Elle-E-Kay for links to your favorite retailers where you find more of my books or post a review.

Thank you.
Elle E. Kay
https://www.elleekay.com

About Author

Elle E. Kay lives in Central Pennsylvania. She loves life in the country on her hobby farm with her husband, Joe. Elle is a born-again Christian with a deep faith and love for the Lord Jesus Christ. She desires to live for Him and to put Him first in everything she does.

You can connect with Elle on her website and blog at https://www.elleekay.com/ or on social media:

Facebook: www.facebook.com/ElleEKay7
Pinterest: www.pinterest.com/elleekay7
Instagram: www.instagram.com/elleekay7
Goodreads: www.goodreads.com/author/show/15016833.Elle_E_Kay

I FIRST CAME TO know Jesus as a young teen, but before long I strayed from God and allowed my selfish desires to rule me. I sought after acceptance and love from my peers, not knowing that only God could fill my emptiness. My teen years were full of angst and misery, for me and my family. People I loved were hurt by my selfishness. My heartache was at times overwhelming, but I couldn't find the healing I desperately desired. After several runaway attempts my family was left with little choice, and they put me in a group home/residential facility where I would get the constant supervision I needed.

At that home I met a godly man called 'Big John' who tried once again to draw me back to Jesus. He would point out Matthew 11:28-30 and remind me that all I had to do to find peace was give my cares to Christ. I wanted to live a Christian life, but something kept pulling me away. The cycle continued well into adulthood. I would call out to God, but then I would turn away from Him. (If you read the Old Testament, you'll see that the nation of Israel had a similar pattern, they would call out to God and He would heal them and bring them back into their land. Then they would stray, and He would chastise them. It was a cycle that went on and on).

When I came to realize that God's love was still available to me despite all my failings, I found peace and joy that have remained with me to this day. It wasn't God who kept walking away. He'd placed his seal on me in childhood and no matter how far I ran from Him, **He remained faithful.** When I finally recognized His unfailing love, I was made free.

2 Timothy 2:13

"If we believe not, yet he abideth faithful: he cannot deny himself."

Ephesians 4:30

"And grieve not the holy Spirit of God, whereby ye are sealed unto the day of redemption."

I let myself be drawn into His loving arms and led by His precious nail-scarred hands. He has kept me securely at His side and taught me important life lessons. Jesus has given me back the freedom I had in Christ on that day when I accepted the precious gift He'd offered. My life in Him is so much fuller than it ever was when I tried to live by the world's standards.

I implore you, if you've known Jesus and strayed, call out to Him.

If you've never known Jesus Christ as your personal Lord and Saviour. Find out what it means to have a relationship with Christ. Not religion, but a personal relationship with a loving God.

God makes it clear in His word that there isn't a person righteous enough to get to heaven on their own.

Romans 3:10

"As it is written, There is none righteous, no, not one:"

We are all sinners.

Romans 3:23

"For all have sinned, and come short of the glory of God;"

Death is the penalty for sin.

Romans 6:23

"For the wages of sin is death; but the gift of God is eternal life through Jesus Christ our Lord."

Christ died on the cross for our sins.

Romans 5:8

"But God commendeth his love toward us, in that, while we were yet sinners, Christ died for us."

If we confess and believe we will be saved.

Romans 10:9

"That if thou shalt confess with thy mouth the Lord Jesus, and shalt believe in thine heart that God hath raised him from the dead, thou shalt be saved."

Once we believe He sets us free.

Romans 8:1

"There is therefore now no condemnation to them which are in Christ Jesus, who walk not after the flesh, but after the Spirit."

I hope you'll take hold of that freedom and start a personal relationship with Christ Jesus.

www.ingramcontent.com/pod-product-compliance
Lightning Source LLC
Chambersburg PA
CBHW011508170626
46812CB00009B/3022